Café Antoinette

a novel

GINA M. ANGELONE

© 2015 Gina Angelone

BLUE EYED EDITIONS

All rights reserved. No part of this book may be used or reproduced in any manner whatsoever without written permission except in the case of brief quotations embodied in critical articles and reviews.

Edition ISBNs
Print: 978-0-9861788-0-1
E-book: 978-0-9861788-1-8

Cover design by Dane Swanepoel
Author photograph by Hattie Brown
Book interior design by Morgana Gallaway

This book is a work of fiction. Names, characters, places, and incidents either are products of the author's imagination or are used fictitiously. Any resemblance to actual events or locales or persons, living or dead, is entirely coincidental.

For my mother, Gerri,
who has not stopped cheering me on since day one

And for my sons, Amadeo and Ariano,
who boost my every aspiration

CHAPTER 1

A DEAL WAS MADE. ONE THAT included vows of sanctity and fidelity and undying togetherness. We decided to keep out the line *till death do us part*, finding it morbid, statistically unreliable, and just plain counterintuitive. The deal also included creating a family, which for me was centered around raising my daughter Jacqui, and for Dalton meant issuing his own genetic stamp and placing it on a brand-new baby, fruit of papa's loin.

After nearly four years of marriage and no prodigy, this part of the deal was affecting the rest of the contract.

Resentment and discontent got spit into napkins at the dinner table. Reproachful tones hovered above the bedsheets—an aborted kiss on the cheek, a cold roll to the edge of the king, tugging at the blankets like knaves over turf. Back to back, we faced our own silent precipice before surrendering to another night of fitful sleep. The unsaid, the undone besieged us. It seeped into the morning coffee and was swallowed with a bitter, hollow *thunk*—nothing to absorb its acid consequence. It grew and grew into the unspoken pachyderm in the room, giant ears flapping with sonic urgency as nothing more was argued, nothing more was heard.

But Dalton had other ways to get a point across. He saved himself for day twelve, when we had our best shot at conceiving. He studied my regularities, my rhythms. He'd give me two days of pleasure each month, maybe three, and then hold back the rest of the time. I accepted my role in his power play and complied for the sake of keeping my end of the bargain: the chance to give him a child. After all, a deal was a deal. Sex was sex. And besides, I wasn't necessarily ovulating when he thought I was.

In the beginning, making love with Dalton was elevating. His lean, muscular, athletic body made me forget my insecurities. I was always so plagued by imperfections: my frizzy hair and lanky, untoned frame. Mine was a body that looked good in clothes. But naked, I felt like an oversized child, as if my limbs were still growing and the rest of me couldn't quite catch up. Somehow my paleness felt sheltered by his tawny physique. We fit. And it felt good.

I realized that we would somehow spend the rest of our lives trying to get back to that beginning—those deep kisses and nights of insatiable lovemaking. Because after four years of marriage, our appetite wasn't so ravenous anymore. I would have done anything to feel that original passion again and the strong, silent man from those first indelible moments. Recalling a time when my husband stared at me with unbridled appetite was becoming my salvation, my feast-filled memory during this time of famine. Now his eyes saw me through a filter of failure and unmet desires.

And then there was the matter of the hiss. That extended *fhhhhh* when he was finished, when the deed was done. I was long past expecting any auditory titillation, but the hiss was too much. I just wanted his heavy torso off my flaxen body and to scream. I wanted to release my wild side and not be ashamed to do it with the man I'd married. But he'd always hiss and, once deflated, lay there. Noiseless.

"A human being's larger purpose in the natural order is procreation. No procreation, no evolution." Dalton said this often, as if holding up his failure to a higher standard.

I hated calling it that: *procreation*. It smacked of Christianity and science. I wasn't sure which was less sexy. Either way, I wasn't getting pregnant no matter how full of faith or facts I was at each ovulation cycle. With Jacqui it had been easy. So effortless. Like she'd been conjured in a dream. Intensely focused, excitable, inquisitive, Jacqui viewed her nine-year-old world with a squint in her eye and a million thoughts rolling across her forehead. She seemed to accept nothing at face value: not colors, not the sky, not the rain, not even us. She looked for a reason in everything, and tallied every injustice.

Dalton always said she'd make a terrific trial lawyer one day. But I knew that my daughter was destined for other things and that her vision, her querying soul, would take her far outside the normal spectrum of options. I took pride in knowing that I had something to do with the formation of this fine human being. It was all I needed.

Still, I didn't want to deny Dalton his ultimate wish.

And though my heart was sympathetic, my body lay silent, puffy, noncompliant. I'd wait another month for the defeated look in his eyes. Dalton, always so sure of himself, on top of the world in a fine Italian suit and well buffed, cap-toe shoes. Suddenly naked and undone. Bravado squeezed down to a whimper, a consoling glance with the words *next time* on crestfallen lips. I was beginning to take strange pleasure in that look.

"Maybe we should relax more. There's too much pressure. We should loosen up. Experiment." I looked up at him from my magazine.

"Experiment? What do you have in mind?"

I pointed to a picture.

He chuckled. "Ah, porn for housewives. Well, we're not going to become circus performers, are we?"

"It's just that always trying to have a baby makes sex very unsexy. Don't you think?"

"He's licking jam off her abdomen! It looks ridiculous to me. I'll do whatever you want, but I think our lovemaking is just fine."

"It doesn't have to be jam. . . ." The subject always knocked the heat out of the conversation. The missing baby: It was becoming the carbon monoxide in the air between us, the silent killer.

"What did the doctor have to say, anyway?" His tie un-noosed, his foot slipping out of soft, nubuck loafers.

"She said that since your sperm count was so good, we should get more aggressive with my tests, check out my tubes, then go from there."

"Sounds like a plan. When can we do the first test?"

I wanted to correct his *we*, ask him if any dyes were being injected into his uterus.

"Dalt, it's nearing the end of the semester. Things are crazy. I'm stressed. I'd rather wait until the school year is over."

"But then you and Jacqui will be leaving for France . . ." A kind of urgency, a clock ticking, audible in his voice.

"Well, we can wait another couple months or so, can't we? I mean, I'll be much more relaxed when I get back, and ready to take on a barrage of tests and, most likely, heavy doses of medication. My body needs a break, Dalt." I declined from mentioning my spirit.

He hugged me from behind, wrapping his arms around my waist, giving in. "All right. I suppose we can wait. But just until you get back, okay?"

"Deal." It was always a deal. And as he stood there holding me, I wondered why he didn't bend me over the bathroom counter at that very moment. An unwanted prudishness had crept into the marriage in between fresh linens and ovulation indicators. Cold, slippery tile was no longer an option for unleashing desire. We cut off our meager cuddle like a bad thought disconnecting from a guilty conscience. I glanced over at the bed, ready to swaddle myself in the narrow satisfaction of foreign cotton and memory foam.

"I'm taking a shower. Jacqui asleep?"

"Yep. She had a long day today." My gaze shifted to the op-ed section of the *Times*. The death toll in the Middle East was up. Awful. Still, my impetus was not to repopulate the world.

Shirt cuffs unbuttoned, belt undone. "How was the thing at the French Club?"

"The Belmondo retrospective? Better than I thought."

"Good. I'll get washed up, then you . . ." His custom-made jacket fell across the rose velvet settee. He liked to have sex when we were clean.

"I already showered. I'll be here." Eyes still fixed on the newsprint, trying to conjure up the buff Belmondo heading into the bathroom. A sudden French New Wave fantasy might serve a greater purpose. It would give me something to think about, to hang onto, eyes closed, hands buttressing the headboard, as Dalton pounded away to the same old rhythms.

"I have a good feeling about all this, hon." He stuck his head outside the bathroom door as if to reassure.

Right. A good feeling. I decided to stick with the thought of a hot French thug and his unlikely American girlfriend hawking English newspapers on the streets of Paris in pedal-pushers and flats, waiting for her lawbreaking lover to show up and whisk her away for a steamy liaison. I closed the paper with a cinematic sigh, took off my robe, and waited for my squeaky-clean husband to emerge from the vapors.

CHAPTER 2

"Hey! Luci! Dalton! So great to see you guys! Honey, the Ameses are here!" Shari Miller, exuberant, chirping, called over to her husband Jay, busy pouring cosmos in their high-chintz Scarsdale home.

"Welcome, guys! Let me get you a drink." Jay smiled broadly as he raised the frosted shaker in his hands, looking for sounds of approval.

"I'll just have a beer, Jay. No girlie drinks for me." Dalton laughed before the others and I held my breath to stave off the abrupt avalanche of mirth that would follow.

"Finally, a man after my own heart. Hey, how's it goin'?" Larry Klinger slapped Dalton on the back and handed him a cold one. The two clinked bottles and drank even before Dalton had his coat off. It was like that when the men got together. They feigned camaraderie, mostly in the form of gender divide and jokes about wives.

Mimi Constantin looked over at me with round, innocent eyes.

"How's work going, Luci?" Her head cocked to one side and she squinted, as if work were some distant place she was trying to imagine from long ago and far away.

"My course load is heavier this semester than it was in the fall, but I like the challenge." I stopped myself from sounding too inspired.

The other women had given up their careers to raise kids and remodel homes. Their ability to speak in Colonial color palettes and layered window treatments was enviable; those were languages I didn't speak so fluently. Chats with colleagues on campus were always so full of wit and reference. This was my chance to wallow in the mundane. I scooped up a passing cosmo and plopped onto the puffy couch with burgundy English setters printed on it. "Mimi, are those Shari's new drapes? They're beautiful. Don't you think?"

"I have a surprise guest for everyone tonight!" Shari scurried across the high-shine wood floors, clicking her way to the appetizers.

"Who's coming? Do you know?" Marilyn Mizner waved her toothpick at her husband Stephen and swallowed hard on a shrimp croquette.

"How should I know? Ask her." Stephen blocked the onslaught of questions with an upheld hand—the hand of someone who never did a day of hard work in his life, the hand of gentry.

"Well," said Marilyn, "are you going to tell us who it is or do we have to liquor you up to get the answer?"

Shari burst out laughing in a way only a hostess can—a laugh that makes everyone feel special, almost coddled in delight for no apparent reason. "Actually, let me start off by saying that I think our own Mrs. Luci Ames will be particularly pleased by these invitees!" Shari's pursed lips and raised eyebrows were almost too much to bear.

Heads darted from Shari to me as I buried my face in my cosmo, looking for oxygen in the vodka and triple sec.

"Well, you all know Francine Clébert . . ." Shari made sure to not pronounce the T, but the name came out like *Clay Bear* anyway, sounding more like pottery and children's books.

"Oh, yeah. Isn't she the one who makes all those phenomenal pastries at Café Antoinette? I love the *milles feuilles*." Marilyn popped another croquette and brandished her plastic toothpick.

I knew Café Antoinette well, but had never sampled the *meal foy*, as Marilyn called it.

"Yes! That's the one! I hope Francine brings her napoleon tonight. I know I shouldn't say that, but I hope she does!" Shari crossed her diamond-studded fingers.

"It depends how hard you dropped the hint, dear. And I do believe I heard something crashing to the floor when you spoke to her the other day." Another big laugh came from Jay and the circle of men tugging on domestic beers with no understanding of fine French pastry.

"Anyway, I'm sure you'll all like the Cléberts. And Luci can jabber away in French because I understand that Francine's husband doesn't speak much English at all. Now, isn't that just the sexiest thing ever?"

The women raised their glasses in full agreement while the men tried out their best French accents on the crudest lines they could muster. I pictured a room full of middle-aged Frenchmen yelling vulgarities in English while standing around a bourgeois dinner party. The thought made my cocktail dribble.

My own French connection was making me more desirable at these events. The monoglots of Scarsdale seemed to have a secret longing to lay claim to something or someone French. It was as if my pale thinness and impeccable accent somehow elevated me to a more moneyed crowd. Teaching Spanish would never have the same inroads in this town.

The doorbell rang and the wives automatically moistened their lips while the men yelled, *"Ze dar! Get ze dar, sumbuddy!"*

Jay wiped the cold sweat of the beer bottle from his hands and went for the handle. Francine Clébert stood there in a skinny black leather jacket and tight jeans, holding forth a large white box with her pastry-shop logo on it: a fancy cursive *CA* sitting in an Old World cartouche. Jay awkwardly planted platonic kisses on both of her sallow cheeks while the big box with its fragile contents floated between them. Shari rushed over and peered in.

"Napoleon! Francine! You shouldn't have!" She turned and winked at the other guests.

Once the pastry box was removed from her thin, bangled arms, Francine was properly introduced to the crowd, everyone trotting out their best *bonjour* or *enchanté* to the new arrival along with the requisite set of pecks on the cheek. The men, in particular, were enjoying the ritual. Shari kept showing off the contents of the box to anyone who'd look, as if unveiling an encounter with the divine.

"You'd think the ol' emperor himself were in that box from the way she keeps bowing to it." Dalton sneered into his drink and I masked my laugh with a cocktail napkin.

"Where's your husband? Won't he be joining us?" Jay temporarily stopped the flow of sweet introductions and confectioned sighs.

"He'll be here in a moment. He had to park the car down the

street." Francine's accent was light and sweet, like her much-anticipated dessert.

"I feel awful! Jay could have parked it for him!" Shari let an exaggerated expression of disapproval linger on her lips.

"Yes, ma'am! I'm Jay the valet!" Jay stood up tall and gave his wife a salute.

A gentle, almost apprehensive knock came from the door and Jay answered with a flourish. *"Entrez!"*

"Didier, viens." Francine waved her husband inside and reinitiated the round of introductions.

"Sorry . . . my English, not so good . . ." The Frenchman looked each person in the eye; smiling, apologetic, guiltless.

I noticed his youthful swagger and cool, urban look—the longer hair that he kept having to sweep back over his face, like he had a constant point to make, the slightly distressed, buttery-looking leather jacket, the thin, black cashmere sweater he wore as a shirt, the clean but well-worn jeans, and the shoes. Dalton was also checking out his shoes: shiny, square-toed, weighty black slip-ons. Stylish. Expensive too. The kind Dalton sold in his store.

"He obviously has time to buy clothes. Why doesn't he have any time to learn English?" Dalton muttered through the side of his mouth, his manicured nails picking the label off his beer bottle. He became more judgmental whenever another good-looking man was in the room.

"That's not fair of you. You go to France all the time and you can barely order a sandwich." I kept my eyes on the new arrival.

"That's because I have you, my dear. And what would I do without you?" He slipped his hand in mine and squeezed it tightly as Didier strode over with our hostess.

"These are the Ameses, Luci and Dalton. Luci is a professor of French over at the university. You two should have lots to talk about!" Shari once again winked, as if cuing me to speak French.

I obeyed, extracting my hand from Dalton's grip and handing it to the Frenchman. His cologned skin smelled of lemongrass and lavender and his scent relaxed me at once.

"Please let me know if there's anything I can help translate for you tonight, although you may have a desirable advantage in not understanding a word."

Didier smiled with raised eyebrows, like he'd just been dealt a full house.

Dalton dug both hands in his pants pockets, looking for another judgment to pull out. None came. I inhaled deeply, as if Jean-Paul Belmondo himself had just walked in the room and asked me for a light.

Francine joined the trio and I initiated the polite inquisition that was expected in such circumstances. Her smile was sheer and watery, like the rest of her, but her eyes showed something more expansive as she looked over at her husband. I tried to perceive the torrent of possibilities within this slight woman—some fatter, inner beauty.

I pointed toward Shari, still hovering over the cake box. "It seems you're already enjoying a great reputation in this town."

Francine squeezed her forehead into a question. "So, you have never tried our *patisserie*?"

"I have and it's wonderful. But not your famous napoleon."

"Well, tonight you must. I insist!"

"Of course." I rubbed my palms together, feigning a sweet tooth and the desire for complicity. I wondered if Francine Clébert could be a new friend, or if this taut little woman was only interested in a new client. I would try the eminent napoleon and decide for myself if the baker were worth her weight in puffed pastry.

"I assure you, you will love it," Didier chimed in, as much repeat customer and happy advertiser as supportive spouse.

He seemed much younger than his wife. Better looking too. For some reason, it bothered me. It made me suspicious of them: this ordinary rail of a woman and her youthful, chic husband. Not that Francine was unattractive. Just that she was so painfully thin—a fact that made me also distrust her pastry. How could someone that reedy be a good baker?

A piercing crystal bell sounded, Shari briskly tolling it through the living room in a strut that seemed more appropriate for herding cattle than calling guests to the table. *"À table! À table! Tout le monde!"*

Francine echoed the hostess's call with a joyful and compliant *"Alors, à table!"* She seemed to know that this whole evening was for her benefit. The big, white cake box with its flowing cartouche said it all, like an open invitation to impress.

"Tonight, husbands and wives will sit separately. You see each other enough, right? And it's boy-girl, boy-girl, of course. Which means Larry and Jay cannot sit together. Sorry guys! Just look for the place setting with your name on it!" Shari Miller was bloated with self-satisfaction.

The dining table was set with shiny silver-leaf chargers under each porcelain plate, like a lunar system of empty moons had revolved around the house and landed peacefully there. Dozens of votive candles adorned the windowsills and threatened the lives of the window treatments. A large candelabra sat in the middle of the table where the floral arrangement usually stood, but which had been relegated to the grand piano for greater effect.

I found my hand-calligraphied place card in periwinkle blue with silvery ink, and felt a slight wince in my gut. It was the same nauseous inferiority I always felt at such events. I barely had enough time to make a proper meal for Jacqui and Dalton, let alone throw a lavish dinner party with handmade place cards. Why were Dalton and I invited to these things when we never reciprocated? How could we? Our lives were much too busy. My china was mix-matched, my cooking skills bleak, and I had only the dullest place mats. I stared at the empty moon in front of my setting and knew that whatever delicacy was coming to fill it would not satisfy my own gnawing inadequacy.

"Ah, they must have put me here to bother you all night. You seem to be my designated translator. It will give Francine a break, at least. As long as you don't mind . . . ." His low, hushed French came as a balm.

I looked up into the pleasant face of Didier Clébert. *"Pas du tout."*

"Everybody have a seat and we'll serve the *potage*." Shari was making a real show of it.

"Oooo la-la, le potage!" Jay jumped in once again with his haughty, mock-French, causing everyone to laugh. Even the Cléberts.

"We are used to it." Didier shrugged, no sign of contempt, and took a sip from his glass.

The evening ensued with light conversation around a heavy meal. Goose-liver pâté with escargot in buttery garlic sauce to begin, then beef bourguignon in a rich red-wine sauce atop a pile of thick noodles. I lost count of how many types of wine were opened and poured. Jay introduced a new vintage for each course, tipping his beak into the goblet for a long, orgasmic inhale, followed by a deft swish before the dark liquid ever neared his tongue. The others tried the same. The more they imbibed, the more sensual and ritualistic the preamble became.

"It's that sommelier class he's taking at the Alliance Française. He's turning into such a connoisseur," Shari bragged.

"Our wine intake has tripled. I want to try everything. The neighbors must think we're a couple of lushes. You should see our bins on recycling day!" Jay's pleasure increased with every bottle he decanted. "The endorphins in this one will blow your socks off. They call it 'the opiate of the masses . . . .'" A 1999 Pinot was ceremoniously uncorked, accompanied by a long *ahhhhh*.

"Here's to fine lushes, good friends, and plenty more dopamines!" Larry raised his glass in a toast. The table echoed with cheers. Clearly, I wasn't the only one seeking comfort in all the emptiness; everyone had some deeper ache they wanted blocked, and the endorphin-filled wine was doing the trick.

Mimi Constantin's big eyes suddenly looked as heavy as saucepans. Her husband John kept poking her in the shoulder and telling her to stay awake, that she was the designated driver that night. I couldn't imagine either one of them behind the wheel, her dozing, him poking. Even the Mizners, the more they drank, acted less annoyed with one another and more lascivious. Stephen's gentrified hands roamed all over Marilyn, sliding down to her buttocks from time to time for a quick squeeze. I couldn't decide which way I liked them less: sober and nagging or drunk and horny.

"Hey, Mizners. Get a hotel room!" Larry Klinger let out a greasy laugh full of red sauce and drowning in butter. His wife Georgina gave him a scolding look but then burst out laughing along with him.

I periodically updated Didier on the goings on and what typical nonsense was being said. Francine laughed with the crowd, complimenting Jay on his fine grasp of wine and Shari for the honor she paid to Burgundy, which was, of course, her region of origin.

"Are you from La Bourgogne too?" I inspected Didier more closely, looking for signs of Gallic provinciality.

"No. I'm Parisian, completely. How boring, no?" His irony didn't seem to carry the faintest sign of inebriation. Just a deep tint of purple on his lips and tongue, like it had been painted there by a Fauvist.

"Paris is a marvelous city. So beautiful, so cultivated . . ." I suddenly felt stupid. Cliché. I couldn't stop thinking about his purple lips.

"Ah, but you have New York. The center of the world. I'm enjoying so much photographing here. Every frame is an entire story, a universe. I love it."

"You're a photographer?" I took another sip of the burgundy wine and tried not to stare at his tongue.

"Yes. A photojournalist, actually. In between assignments, I like to do my own work. The city has been a superb tableau for me."

"What do you normally photograph?"

"Wars. I've spent the past decade shooting mainly in Africa. Both in the Muslim nations and black Africa. I love it there. More than anywhere."

I suddenly felt as superfluous and overdone as Shari Miller's drapes. Here was someone who stepped into war, suffused himself in it, captured its pains and suffering, lived life outside of the living. Or so I imagined. I was filled with an urge to ask him things. About what he saw and felt and witnessed. About bloodshed and violence and fear. And how can he breathe in a room full of drunken Americans when so many people are dying in the world. I opened my mouth to speak, but the purple stains across his mouth, his youthfulness and handsome face, made me lose my train of thought.

"Hon, lay low on the wine. Remember what the doctor said. You should be as healthy as possible." Dalton was a little late with his prescription.

"And now, it's the time we've all been waiting for: the napoleon!" Shari seemed to have been holding her breath the whole dinner, just waiting to puncture the inflated dessert.

Everyone clapped and Francine waved off the applause with visible embarrassment. Didier curled his lips in an expression of pride, but from the side, it looked like something else. Like a thought was perched under all the sugarcoating.

The small Tiffany chinaware plates were passed around, each bearing a generous portion of the flaky dessert. There was no getting back to my conversation with Didier, no asking about life or death or anything of consequence. Puff pastry was the only topic of conversation, and it trotted around the table like the great emperor and his horse tearing through the Alps. I took a small bite and gave an appreciative—if not exaggerated—nod to Francine. But my thoughts kept turning toward the Frenchman and his empty plate. His violet lips and tongue. His dusty wars. And black Africa, the place he loved more than anywhere. I hoped to see him again when normal color would return to our complexions and ask him why. Why Africa? Why war? And why wasn't he having any dessert?

CHAPTER 3

DALTON SLIPPED INTO HIS pointed, goatskin oxfords and tied the thin brown laces, giving an extra tug to make sure the bow sat just right and wouldn't come undone. It was a gesture he'd made a million times. Unconscious. Automatic. Like the way he kissed me good-bye before dashing out the door. A quick peck on the left cheek, his skin smelling of verbena and spice. There were no loose ends about him.

"How about the three of us go for sushi tonight?" He dusted a fleck of white from his dark English suit.

"I love sushi!" Jacqui shaped her hands into circles as if summoning up a plate of perfect geometric things.

"I can't believe you can think about food after a dinner like that. I'm still full." The aftereffects of excessive wine and beef bourguignon were still coursing in my bloodstream.

"Yeah, but you won't be full at seven PM and I want to eat light tonight."

"Sure. Jacqui and I can pick you up at the train and we'll go from there."

"Perfect. Dinner with my two girls and *unagi maki*. What could be better? Come on, kiddo. Let's go."

"Bye, Mama!" Jacqui picked up her backpack and leaned in for a hug.

Dalton pecked my cheek, waving his newspaper over his head, and set out into the day, impeccable, pinstriped, fragrant. Automatic.

Dalton: The same sweet-smelling man I'd always known. Had anything about his manicured demeanor changed in all these years? I couldn't think of a thing. No, Dalton had definitely remained the same: satisfied by his privileged status, happy at work and blessed with good looks, a fine imported wardrobe, a fit physique. He had it all. Except the baby. The monthly minus, like a report card denoting his one spectacular failure.

I combed back my shock of hair into its signature chignon. It was a look that suited: secure and tame. But on this particular day it seemed wrong. I needed something different, something unrestrained, less severe. A change. I yanked out the familiar bun and the unmanageable hair hung loose. It wasn't so bad. It framed my face nicely, landing softly on the shoulders. It was too wavy, certainly, but it had a bouncy feminine quality that was almost admirable. I reached for a dark lipstick, rolling a deep layer across my lips. The bruised color of it reminded me of Didier Clébert.

I couldn't imagine photographing war. Risking one's life for art. Not many people could do it. My curiosity was definitely piqued. I wanted to see those photos. I wanted to see him, or maybe invite him to show his work at the French Club. He could give a talk, answer some questions. It would offer a nice change from all the film screenings and food events. I would call Shari right away, thank her for the indulgent evening, and get the Clébert's number.

A key turned in the latch of the vestibule door. "Hello, Miss Luci. It's me," Norma called up the stairs.

"Hi, Norma. I'm just getting dressed. I'll be down to make some fresh coffee in a moment."

"Take your time. I already had some this morning. Let me start down here, okay?" The vacuum and the bucket of cleaning supplies were dragged from the broom closet through the house on their usual pilgrimage. The ritual sounds of Monday morning began and the drone set me strangely on edge.

I checked myself out in the mirror and saw something more reckless and alive. As the hum of housecleaning began, I imagined a thousand rash thoughts, a war-torn landscape, a photo exhibit, and the indelible stain of wine.

CHAPTER 4

It was already past one o'clock when I hurried from my office to the university parking lot. I signaled Sabine through her windshield. She nodded, slathering her hands in anti-bacterial soap, then rolled down the window and checked her face in the rearview mirror.

"Sorry I'm late, Sabine. You're flushed. You feeling okay?"

"Yeah, doll, I'm great. Just a little phone sex with Omar. I should have left the engine running; I needed the air." She fanned her face as if drying her fingernails.

"You had phone sex here? In the university parking lot?" I took a step back, not wanting to get too close to the mingling smells of hormones, Crystal, and new leather interiors.

"Well, I got here a few minutes early. He called, so I figured, Why not? So . . . you hungry or what, because I'm famished." Sabine licked her glossy lips.

"Yes, but unfortunately, I don't have time to leave campus today. We'll have to grab something at the commissary."

"Do you have a class or something?"

"No, no. I have a meeting."

"You mean I left poor Omar with a stiffy so you and I could do a quickie at the cafeteria? Tragic: coitus interruptus and institutional dining."

"Sorry, girlfriend. You can have all the salad bar you want. Can't help you with the other part, though."

Sabine stepped out of the car, all legs and heels, shifting her bust line into place, and smoothing out her waist. "Say there, *chica*, you look extra good today. I'm loving the hair au naturel."

I gave my loose curls a squeeze. "Thanks. Just a little change I made. Whenever I wear it down, Dalton thinks I look like a mop."

"Ugh. Dalton. Tell him to stick to the feet. Your head looks just fine. I swear, that husband of yours is so . . . *missionary* pose."

"Thanks."

"You're welcome, sweetie. Now let's eat. Do they have make-your-own-sundaes at this joint?"

As we walked through the quadrangle over to the dining hall and through the lost temptations of the salad bar, I felt strangely excited about my upcoming meeting with Didier Clébert. He'd sounded genuinely enthusiastic when I called earlier and asked if I could see his work. I liked his voice. It was quiet and gracious, as if he actually reflected before he spoke.

CAFÉ ANTOINETTE

"Omar was like a dog in heat last night. I'm sore, actually." Sabine stabbed at her Caesar with exaggerated effort.

"Sabine! People can hear you!"

"Good. I'm sure they could learn a few things. At least I'll give Omar that: He knows what a woman wants. And you, my dear? You two still hammering away at repopulating Scarsdale?"

A forkful of field greens fell back on my plate. No appetite.

"I'll take that as a *yes*. Well, there's nothing that kills a sex life more than reproduction. It's so clinical."

"Tell me about it. It's like he's creating a trademark or something."

A flip of bleached hair. A long, reflective sip of diet soda. "I'm so glad my two boys are grown and out of the house. I bet I'm having more sex than both of them combined."

"Divorce seems to be suiting you just fine. You've never looked better."

"Thanks, doll. Frankly, I recommend it to any woman married to a schmuck for as long as I was." Sabine lifted her glass like a lady, gingerly, by the stem. "Here's to getting shtupped on a regular basis!"

"To getting shtupped. Listen, this afternoon, there's part two of a Belmondo retrospective at the French Club and I'm moderating. If you've got nothing to do, you're welcome to come."

"Belmondo? Wasn't he that lady-killer from the sixties with the dark hair and the punched-in schnoz? Now there's a man who knew how to do it." Sabine traced a finger under her soft brown eyes, lightly smearing her dark eyeliner and acquiring a sudden smoldering look. "Lord, he must be as ugly as a lizard by now. . . ."

"He's actually not that much older than you."

"But has he had the work done that I've had? And by the finest hands in New York?" Sabine dramatically raised her jeweled fingers to frame her attractive profile.

"No one looks as good as you, girlfriend."

"I know, sweetie. I'd love to see you do your stuff in the classroom and watch old movies with a French hottie, but I've got an afternoon-delight session with Omar. At the construction site." She worked away at the croutons. Voracious.

"The construction site?"

"I know. We might bring the whole place down if we're not careful."

"Remember, hard hats do not count as contraception." I planted a light kiss on each of her perfect cheekbones and slid two twenties on the table to cover lunch.

"No, no. You save that for your next box of pregnancy tests."

The irony of our unlikely friendship made me smile, from the first time I saw Sabine in a yoga class wearing her stretchy pants so low that her thong showed whenever she bent over. The other women whispered behind her back, shocked that a woman of her age would wear something so confident and exposed. But I admired her strong physique and stringy underwear. I liked that Sabine was so sensual and hedonistic, that she joked openly about her plastic surgeries, and that she always made an entrance and an exit. Sabine swore that yoga doubled her sex drive. She especially loved the inversion poses.

A Kama Sutra book in fleshy pink paper was her gift to me one Christmas. I made sure to spend time with it prior to my rituals with Dalton. I needed a fresh image to keep me going while he whispered "come on, baby" in my ear before propping my legs above my head for twenty minutes in a fertility rite that not even yoga could have readied me for.

Sabine drove off in the finely made German auto she'd won in her divorce settlement, wiggling her long red nails out the window and speed-dialing Omar. She was someone who knew how to break monotony, how to live. I had my routines. And they fell around me with palpable weight. I could set my clock by them. Almost every moment of my day was planned, programmed, accomplished in a certain way. I hoped Jacqui's life wouldn't become the same. Her abundance of activities was already overtaking the free hours of the week.

If I thought for a moment that having another child would generate a radical disruption to the point of issuing liberation, then I would submit. I would engage in every procedure, scientific and other, to comply and succeed. But there were no assurances. Just a long list of more scheduled activities and an abundance of highly qualified nannies. Which meant that I would most likely keep my post at the university that I'd worked so hard to get and the tenure I fought to ensure, and that some other woman would raise my baby. It meant that a new, enormous set of routines would be inserted into my life. Our lives. And I would rise each day with a smile on my face and love in my heart and die over and over in a thousand small gestures.

I took an opposite path back to my office at Stanley Hall, hoping that the simple action of going off course, off routine, would set in motion a series of unanticipated events. Or maybe just a single random, unplanned act. But there stood the large gray double doors of my building, offering uninterrupted passage to my office. Curriculum papers filled my in-box. Routine is what curriculum becomes when strictly enforced.

There were days when I remembered why I wanted to teach, what excited me so much about it, the challenges of it, the joys of imparting a bit of knowledge to someone else, the tiny light in someone's eyes when this knowledge resonated. The curriculum I preferred would include reading foreign journalism seated in a café, discussing articles and world events while sipping coffee and wiping ink and pastry glaze off of my fingers. My students would agree. But the choice wasn't ours. The French department had its routines and its syllabus.

At five minutes after two, there was a knock on my office door. I knew it was coming, but there was something unanticipated in its arrival. It was light, unimposing. I was expecting a more forthright, interruptive rap. I stood up to answer, suppressing my usual cry of *"Entrez!"* Didier Clébert stood there, dark hair still slightly humid from a recent shower, face rosy from shaving. I greeted him with a customary kiss to both cheeks, noting the pleasant, soapy smell on his skin.

"Glad you could make it. Please, come in." I directed him to the chair facing my desk.

"Yes, well, I'm pleased to be here. Thank you for receiving me. And so quickly."

"Not at all. Can I offer you something to drink? Coffee? Water?"

"No, no. I'm fine." He held his large black leather portfolio on his lap, tapping his fingers lightly across it. "Excuse me, but your hair . . ."

I cocked my head sideways and a frizzy blond curl fell across my face. "Yes?"

"It's changed, no? You were wearing it differently before. It's nice like that."

My hands nervously ran over my head, pushing a few rebel locks behind my ears. "Thanks. It's funny that you noticed."

"I'm a photographer. That's what I do: I notice things." He offered an obvious smile.

I also noticed things. I noticed that his lips were not the same; they were no longer stained with layers and vintages of wine. They were just regular pink lips, rather un-savage and thin, over a lightly caffeine-tainted smile. I felt instantly relieved and only a little bit disappointed. Those lips had been troubling me. Now, I could let them go.

A laugh escaped me. "That's right. You notice things. May I?" I gestured toward his portfolio.

"Absolutely. I brought with me my series on the Algerian civil war. You know, over seventy journalists were killed during this war. I knew some of them. I also brought a photo essay I did during three trips to Congo as well as some images from Rwanda. These are devastating places and what I saw was unimaginable. But while I was photographing, I also had the chance to focus on something else. I will show you."

He unzipped the portfolio and removed a black book of large, plastic-sheaved prints. The first one was a picture of a little boy. He looked destitute and severely emaciated, but his eyes shone like two beautiful orbs.

"His name is Lumumba. It means *gifted* in Congolese."

I stared at the child. "My God, he's so young. He must be seven. Too young to see that much suffering."

"He was thirteen at the time of this picture, actually. No food, no growth." Didier's words came matter-of-factly.

"Did the boy have any family that survived?" I felt like another ignorant white person with distant, morbid curiosity.

"An uncle who worked for the transitional government. But he was of no help. Lumumba became a child soldier. The only way to make it."

"Did he?"

"For a while."

A quiet took over while I carefully looked through the ominous book of photos, each shot centering on the face of a child, the life of a child. Each set of lost eyes and broken stares on a backdrop of social, moral, political decay. Behind them, piles of human corpses, slightly out of focus. Next to them, heaps of refuse and the meager material detritus of empty lives and vacant homes: a jug, a cloth, a bowl, a torn photo. Little heads covered or shaved to avoid disease, badly scarred and full of marks. Small bones popping through every frame, every bit of filthy, tattered clothing exhibiting a distended belly atop a prominent pelvis and matchsticks for legs. Flies hovered on young, full lips where words would never be enough.

"More people died from starvation than massacre in this war. Over five million." He seemed to be studying the expression on my face as I took in every detail.

"It's hard to turn the page . . . like each one deserves more time and more respect."

"They do. They certainly didn't get any in life. My hope is to offer them that chance now, through these portraits."

A slow exhale escaped. My chin rested heavily in my hand. Another boy. His shirt covered in blood, a small baby asleep in a dirty sling around his back.

"That's Mani. His baby sister is dead. He just didn't know it yet."

A small emotion built in my eye.

"It's very powerful, Didier. Frankly, I wasn't quite expecting this."

"Well, it's war, you know. If you prefer, my wife Francine can speak at your event instead. I think most people would much rather talk about cakes and pastries than discuss genocide. I know I would."

My eyes met his. "That's not what I mean. Your work is really beautiful. But I can't separate the quality of the photograph from the subject. And the subject is difficult and gripping and very, very hard on the heart."

"I know. Maybe you've seen enough?"

"No. I'd like to see them all. More time and respect, right?"

I poured over the shots as Didier sat back in his chair, giving information about each child's name, age, and what happened to his or her village. On more than one occasion, I discreetly wiped away a tear. My newly cascading hair was good for that: shielding a true view of things.

"I see these pictures and I think of my own child. My daughter Jacqui. She's only nine. I can't imagine her surviving anything like this. Do you have any children?"

He slipped a little deeper into his jacket. "No, no. Francine works too much and me . . . well, I don't know. I just don't know about bringing a child into this world. I've seen the worst of it."

I'd heard people express this kind of opinion before and generally regarded it as an excuse, a stalling tactic, a loveless rationale for being too selfish. After all, the ones who said this were not living in constant warfare or in destitution and poverty with no means out. They were in New York, leading privileged lifestyles that they didn't wish to compromise. They blamed the ozone layer, pesticides, and bombs in faraway places for not wanting children. They thought the world was too scary a place for innocence. But Didier was different. He knew the world in all its ugliness. He saw it and lived it. He looked in the eyes of these dejected human beings and lost a bit of hope for humanity. That, I understood.

And yet it also came as a huge relief. Yes, a relief that a man, any man, would not want to leave his mark and procreate. Dalton would think him absurd, unevolved. But I found the idea immeasurably sane.

"I wish I could have brought even one child back with me from Congo. Just one. To know you've saved one life would give meaning to everything, no? But I couldn't. It was impossible at the time. Impossible." He repeated the word as if to convince himself of it.

I didn't have to ask; I knew how painful it would be to bond with these children, however briefly, and then abandon them. It seemed infinitely cruel that they would spend the rest of their short lives being forsaken over and over and over again. I thought of Jacqui, and how she cried whenever a friend left her out of a game or when she missed a sleepover party. That was the depth of my daughter's pain in her young, overprotected life. Jacqui needed to see these pictures. Jacqui needed to see.

"Listen, Didier, it would be my honor to present you and your photos at our event."

"You sure you don't want the cakes? As you've seen, they make for abundantly happier conversation. . . ."

"I do want the cakes. But I want the photos first. Agreed?"

"Agreed."

CAFÉ ANTOINETTE

I paused, a sudden impulse tugging at me as I tossed my hair freely to the side. "There's a Belmondo retrospective starting on campus in fifteen minutes, if you care to join me."

His eyebrow raised and smile widened. "Belmondo?" He stood and reached for the door, giving way to temptation. "After you . . ."

CHAPTER 5

Norma picked up the glass slipper and caressed it the same way she did every time she cleaned. More than once she seemed tempted to try it on, slide her foot gently into the coolness of it. But I guessed that she didn't want to risk cracking the fine crystal, or worse, getting her foot stuck inside. She knew the slipper was a perfect size seven and that she was an eight. Still, I could always tell by the way she held it that she desperately wanted to squeeze into it. She focused all her care and attention on the finely crafted shoe. It seemed that she actually looked forward to dusting it each week, wiping it with a special cleaner and rubbing it with a soft cloth as if it were the prettiest thing she'd ever seen.

"Damn, she's got it good!" The words escaped her as she rubbed, like a thought-bubble popping above her head.

I softly padded over to where she stood. "Did you say something, Norma?"

Her hands fumbled, nearly losing her grip on the slipper. "You scared me, Miss Luci!"

"Sorry, I didn't mean to. I thought I heard you saying something."

"Oh, I was just admiring this." She held the glass shoe up to the light like a prism. "It's so beautiful. So special. That Mr. Ames sure is romantic, no?"

"Mmmmm." I contemplated Dalton's planned, monthly baby-making sessions and all the motions of rigorous, dispassionate sex. How romantic.

"Well, I sure don't know any other woman who got a glass slipper for her engagement, do you?" Norma seemed to be insisting.

"No, I don't. But then again, Mr. Ames is in the shoe business." I didn't want to smear Norma's crystalline view of things, but a point was to be made.

"Still, it's so . . . different."

I knew what Norma meant. I remembered how I felt the moment Dalton offered me the exquisite shoe on a pale-blue satin pillow. He slipped it onto my foot like Prince Charming himself, down on one knee, caressing my heel in his hand. I was a bundle of nerves, thrilled, embarrassed, overwhelmed. The shoe, of course, was a perfect fit. Dalton simply said, "I knew it. You're the one I've been searching for," as if he'd been practicing those words for all of his professional life. Then he pulled a black velvet ring box from his pocket, a large emerald-cut diamond inside, and asked me to marry him, to spend the rest of my life with him. And I said *yes*. All trembly and unworthy, I said yes.

He was a knight in shining armor, rescuing the frantic, exhausted, single mother from a four-story, walk-up apartment in lower

Manhattan. He was all movie-star looks and noble intentions. He came with the big, fine house in the excellent school district, a well-appointed life, a secure sense of self. He was solid. I was liquid and drowning. I took his hand and blissfully voyaged toward my new life as Mrs. Dalton Ames.

It's just that now, things were a bit . . . different.

"It's true, Norma. Mr. Ames does lots of special things."

"And if you don't mind me saying, he's so handsome too. You're lucky, Miss Luci. Lucky as a dog."

"You don't say?" My nose twitched at the comparison.

Norma blew a gust of hot breath on the crystal slipper and admired its sparkle.

Poor Norma. If the slipper didn't hold such sentimental value, I'd almost consider giving it to her.

I headed toward the front door, slipping into my flats and questioning for a second if Dalton were being withheld some well-deserved adulation. Maybe he was.

CHAPTER 6

THE 1960S BRICK STRUCTURE OF Woodside Elementary stood momentarily quiet, waiting for the predictable gush of children to issue from its large red doors. Moms in stretchy workout wear juggled extra-tall lattes and colorful cell phones, congregating around the fence like they were waiting for reservations. As if they were already on their way to somewhere better.

They waved long, painted nails at one another and complimented each other's figures, while everyone insisted they were still too fat, or not as thin as last year, or had lost too much muscle tone after the vacation in the Caribbean because you know how much they make you eat on those cruises.

The women wore designer sunglasses standing in the shade, avoiding eye contact with the small army of nannies shielding the light with their hands and waiting with foreign expressions of servitude to pick up their young charges. I knew these women through their children—the ones in Jacqui's class. We nodded, offering limited, pinched smiles, afraid that something more friendly or judgmental might occur if we attempted to have a conversation.

Children filed out into the parking area with their heads in the sunlight, hair glinting, eyes darting, showing early signs of self-consciousness as they approached their mothers. Jacqui skipped into view, long chestnut hair held back in a lavender band, backpack bounding behind her. A wave of something ethereal always overcame me whenever I saw her from afar. Like I had everything and nothing to do with this magnificent little being.

"Hi, Mama." Jacqui lifted her face to receive a kiss.

"Hey, babe. How was your day?"

"Good." She latched onto my arm.

The other moms noticed our easy affection, their own children bustling into the lot, poised to shun the oncoming gloss and embrace.

"Ready to go ice-skating, then?" I squeezed Jacqui in close at my side.

"Yes! Are you going to skate today or watch?"

"I think I'll sit it out today, if you don't mind. I'd rather watch you."

"Cool. I'm working on my waltz jump this week." Jacqui sprung into a leap, making a half revolution in the air and landing on her opposite foot.

"That'll be impressive on the ice."

"Yeah, it's really hard, but I can almost do it."

"Show me again."

Jacqui leaped her way back to the car, arms outstretched, counting her steps, one-two-three, limbs and hair trailing behind her, yelling "today's the day!"

The rink sucked the spring air out of the afternoon, like a switch being thrown on winter; it was instantly wooly and frosty again. The brisk temps set everything on edge. Even Jacqui seemed rattled as she madly fished her skating gear out of the bag.

"I've got to hurry! See you, Mama!"

"Have fun!"

There were only a few skaters out on the ice. The open session was taking place on a second rink. I stole a peek at the mad whoosh of people, the tiny tots with arms and legs akimbo, making their way fearlessly round and round with the bigger, faster skaters while the *thud* of bass-driven pop blared from the rink's old speakers. I usually enjoyed being in the crowd, slowly winding my way round the giant oval, making small turns and jagged stops, imagining that I could do more, or that a sudden ability would allow me, one day, to fly over the ice. But fear always got in the way of my imaginary leaps and turns. One perfect leap: That was all I wanted.

Coffee in hand, I settled into the hard bleachers that surrounded the practice rink as Jacqui took her warm-up tours. She seemed so confident on the slippery surface, so much in control. I envied her boldness and grace and wondered how a child of mine could be so adroit.

A young couple took the ice in the far corner to work on their routine. Their coach, in her long, quilted-down coat, was a stark contrast to the thinly-clad couple. The coach cued up the music. I recognized the tune: It was the theme song to the film *A Man and a Woman*. The cliché of it almost made my coffee topple. Surely, they were too young to know the movie or even appreciate it. Still, the choice was admirable, sentimental as it was.

Watching the advanced skaters was always a treat. Especially the ones who made everything look so effortless and free, as if they lived on some elevated plane where life floated and sashayed. It was like witnessing a spectacular flying dream. This young couple was particularly good, drawing perfect trails around the rink, their bodies lean and strong, their faces clear and compelling. It seemed more than just an athletic undertaking for them: There was a chemistry that was apparent. The way they held their glances in each other's eyes, the way their hands sought out each other's fingertips.

While the coach addressed them and corrected their timing, the young man wrapped his arm around his partner's waist as if propping her up. She simply leaned in closer and smiled. The more I watched them, the more I realized they were constantly touching, as if they couldn't let go of their connection. Even after he threw her into a release, they found each other quickly, mirroring each other's movements fluidly, easily. The music played on and their figures glided dramatically across the ice, filling me with a hovering sense of melancholy. Young love and French film scores could do that to a person.

In one final gesture to culminate the end of the routine, he lifted her up over his head, her body elegantly stretched out like a halo above him, and spun her around as if worshipping her very being. Then, in a swift and deft movement, he folded her down into his arms as she slid into a perfect split at his feet, hugging his calf in adoration, while he searched the invisible skies above for strength. The dramatic end of the routine appeared as open to conjecture as the future love life of the two protagonists. Both in the film and on the ice. Either way, it was breathtaking.

Maybe it was the sublime exhibit of human potential, like watching a paraplegic cross the finish line in a marathon, or maybe it was the sad swell of reminiscent sound from the boom box, or even the cold air hitting me square in the face. But whatever it was, I suddenly realized that tears were squiggling down my cheeks.

The sound of Jacqui's skates cutting into the ice reached me before my daughter did. "So Mama, did you see? Did you see that last one? It was a perfect waltz jump! I did it!"

"Oh, honey, I'm so sorry. I got distracted. I missed it. Can you do it again for me?" I looked sympathetically into her eyes, quietly dabbing my face with my palms.

"Mama? What's wrong? Why are you crying?"

"It's nothing. I just—I just thought of something. That's all."

"Something bad?"

"No, sweetie, it was actually something good. Now, go on: Do your waltz jump again. For me."

"Okay, but watch me this time. I don't know if it can be so perfect the second time around."

Jacqui regained the ice, her coach urging her on with a few helpful reminders. A moment later, her small feet took to the air, landing with a slight wobble on the finish. I stood up and applauded.

"I told you! It was so much better the first time!" she called out from across the rink.

It always was.

The pair of young skaters exited the ice and I couldn't help but spy on their affections. The young man covered his partner with a warm jacket, then got down on his knees and untied her skates, pulling them off one by one, rubbing her feet to warm them. The young woman seemed to expect his attention, but melted into his gestures nonetheless, offering coy, entitled smiles, stroking his head from time to time, as if to reciprocate something she couldn't express.

The kneeling made me think of Dalton: his proposal, the glass slipper, and Norma's reaction that afternoon. Maybe when Norma held the slipper, she felt the same sentiment I did while watching these skaters. Maybe it wasn't about romance or passion or the potential for desire, but about longed-for things we never quite attain because we're so afraid of falling or getting hurt or crashing into someone.

Jacqui arrived off-rink, skating gear in hand while the noisy Zamboni cleaned the ice for the next practice team, erasing the beautiful circles in the surface and clearing the slate of all of its relevance, all of its story. As we headed out the door into the early spring evening, I removed my thick sweater, feeling the sharp pinch of missing warmth.

My bag dropped on the living-room couch and I wanted to land there with it. The gloom had not yet lifted. Not really.

"Jacqui, go do your homework before dinner. We have to pick up Daddy in an hour."

She obediently dragged her backpack into the kitchen, turning on the light. "Is it okay if I have a snack?"

Part of me wanted to tell her to indulge in cake before dinner. I wanted to be that mother.

"Why don't you have an apple?"

A glint on the mantel caught my eye, and for the first time in a long time, I went over and took the crystal slipper down from its perch. As I sat down and removed my flats, my left foot slid carefully, preciously into the glass. It felt just as I'd remembered, cool and sharp and weighty. I liked the feeling. But something was wrong.

I took off my thin black sock and tried again. Still, my foot was too wide for the shoe. No matter how I tried, it felt tight. An unwarranted panic rose inside. This was ridiculous. The shoe was custom-made for me. What could have happened? Feet don't just get bigger or wider. Do they? This shoe was supposed to fit forever. It had to. Otherwise, it was just a shiny memory on the mantel, a sad, indulgent reminder of what was meant to be, the story I was supposed to have. I prodded and squeezed, but my foot would not fit the shoe correctly. I suddenly felt like an overgrown, ugly stepsister.

"Mama?" Jacqui's voice called out from the kitchen. "Can I eat that creamy, puffy thing in the fridge?"

The doled-out leftovers of Francine Clébert's idyllic dessert.

"No, sweetie, you can't."

"But I want it." Her plea filled with longing.

"I know, dear. But you can't have it."

The sound of the refrigerator suctioned closed, my daughter's hunger left unfulfilled, guarded behind magnets and taped-up snaps of happy times. As I lingered on the plush seat cushion, unable to fathom exactly what had happened and when, it occurred to me with terrible regret that perhaps passion—like the kind in movies and fairy tales and untarnished young couples—might never, ever come my way again.

CHAPTER 7

Café Antoinette had a certain authenticity, which the denizens of Scarsdale greatly appreciated. Though the establishment was completely new, it had the look and charm of the Old World, and felt as if consular approval were needed to enter—an elitism that came with living in that particular zip code. No one really wanted to patronize a place that smelled musty or seemed in great need of window cleaner. They wanted the Old World package dressed up in shiny granite countertops, served with high-design bowls and ergonomic spoons. Classic on the outside and painstakingly modern on the inside. This was, after all, how they viewed themselves.

The people of the village knew good taste when they saw it or when it was marketed correctly and sold to them at elevated costs. Tudor homes were everywhere, as if the original English settlers had passed an edict on architecture. There were fine lace and wine shops, antique furnishings, and dense fabric boutiques in which to swathe the home or wrap oneself up like a tailor-made coat of arms.

"*Un croissant au buerre et un grand café crème, s'il vous plaît.*" I ordered my continental breakfast from the young bakery employee transported from France on a temporary work visa.

The high engine of the espresso maker kept the place revving. The well-lit displays made the pastry seem more like fine jewelry and the indulgence of choosing one or two all the sweeter. The baguettes came in *moelle* for soft and chewy, or *croquante* for crunchy, and for its vast selection of bread alone, Café Antoinette stood out as a beacon of diversity in a sea of enriched white emptiness of Westchester County.

The order came up and I took a seat in the small cane-backed chair and the black-and-white marbletop café table, furnishings that recalled the style and grace of the famous cafés in Paris along the Boulevard Montparnasse and St. Germain: La Coupole, Café Lipp, Aux Deux Magots. The only thing missing were the luminaries. Instead of Picasso or Hemingway or Gertrude Stein, there were Shari Miller and the ladies from the Pilates class stopping by for a coffee klatch before hitting the gym. I pictured a Paris salon full of artists and intellectuals in spandex lying on the floor and lifting their legs in large swooping circles left and right.

"Luci! What a nice surprise! Don't you just love this place? It's a haven." Shari leaned over my table, tight gym clothes clinging to her pear-shaped body. The other ladies in her entourage stepped up to the display to gaze at the exquisite temptations they'd most certainly have to account for with many more hours of unpleasant exertion. Instead, they ordered large, foamy coffees and small madeleines with exaggerated looks of longing—looks that I could relate to, looks that said, "What you want is right in front of you, but you can't have it." They would have to accept their small, spongy cookies and me, my unnamed desire for something bigger than what Café Antoinette could offer that morning.

"Off to the gym, Shari?" My thoughts got buried in the thick foam of the *grand crème*.

"Gotta work off those dinner parties, right?" Shari tapped my shoulder with her cluster of rings, making a slight imprint on my sweater. "Well, you're so thin, you never have to work out."

"I'd love to exercise. It's just I have no time."

"I understand . . ." Shari's mind already drifting to some other distant sympathy. "You guys will have to come over again soon."

"Yes. That would be lovely." A smile stretched out and held its place, least I appear unfit or insincere.

Shari raised her hand close to her face, mouthing the words *bye-bye* on peachy lips.

I sank deeper into breakfast, dunking one end of the croissant into the coffee and savoring a taste that made me close my eyes and issue a small, involuntary sigh. It lifted me outside my suburban confines and left me mouth-agape on the corner of a small street in the sixth arrondissement. After the second dip, I sensed the most meager of shadows by my side. I looked up and saw the slender frame of Francine Clébert, white cuffs upturned over a soft sweater, hands posed confidently on slim, willowy hips.

"*Alors* . . ." A smile emerged on her face like a magician who'd just turned the perfect sleight of hand.

Was it the heat from the coffee or being exposed in a moment of pleasure that changed my color to crimson? I straightened. "*Bonjour*, Francine."

"Nice to see you. Enjoying your breakfast?"

"As you can see . . ."

"Good. Our *croissant au buerre* won awards three years in a row in Paris. There are no such awards here, but anyway, it's good to know there's a heritage, no?" Francine tapped the menu, exhibiting a golden circle of laurels framing the year and the named prize. Certainly, it was no small thing to claim such an award in Paris where the competition was so dense. I nodded respectfully.

Francine Clébert knew well her place in the world, the way celebrities and blue bloods do. She needed no false exaltation. "I heard you have seen Didier's photographs?"

"Yes, yes. I did. They're quite wonderful. It'll be such a big treat for us to exhibit them at the French Club. We're so glad he's agreed to do it."

Francine bent silently into the café chair, like a bow over a cello. "Didier has so much talent, so much to offer. His photographs are hard to look at. It's so sad, the things that he has seen. Impossible, really."

"Yes."

Francine's laurelled universe of confections was a strange counterpoint to her husband's unsweetened worldview.

"Of course, Francine, we'd be equally honored to have you come speak at the French Club. What you do is also interesting, and if there's a family heritage involved, then I'm sure there's a fascinating story as well."

Francine tilted her head to one side and her short, blunt crop of hair formed a protective shell around her trim face. "I don't know how fascinating it is, but yes, I'm a third-generation *patissier*."

"That's remarkable." A long draw on my coffee.

"Well, the family name is very known in Paris. The prime minister himself only buys our breads. We deliver each morning to his *bureaux*. It was my grandfather's dream to be a great *patissier*. He was absolutely passionate about it. He developed an exact science for each recipe. My father improved on it and then kept the reputation strong."

"And your father still runs the bakery in Paris?"

"My father died five years ago. After that, I wanted to follow my own dream. I sold my half of the bakery to my brother and decided to create my own business."

"Why didn't you stay in Paris?"

"I didn't want to compete with my brother or make bad dynamics in the family. You know, in Paris it's small; people talk. I knew that New York would be the place for me to do something on my own."

"But why here in Scarsdale?"

"The right demographics, incomes, the inclination toward everything French. Plus, Manhattan is prohibitive for me. Maybe in some years we'll be able to open there. I hope."

Francine was right to put her café in the middle of the village of Scarsdale. She could smell the wealth of the people and feel their hunger for finery. This was their respite from the mad sophistication of New York City, where posh French cafés hung a sign on so many corners. But here, the people could drop the chaos and keep the erudition. Here, both Francine and her pastries could rise to the top like a golden, flaky brioche or a prize croissant.

"Well, two lovely ladies catching up, I see." Didier appeared, relaxed, uncombed, *Le Monde* tucked under his arm. He pulled a chair up to the table and delivered light kisses to both of us.

I found myself uncharacteristically drawn to this couple. Their easy chic, their educated charm, their artisanal passion for their work, their light, glib Parisian flare. For a moment, I envied them. My claims to the language were hard-earned and unnatural, my marriage unpeppered with light kisses and pet names. Everything seemed more enticing in their presence. Even breakfast.

"I'd better get back in the kitchen." Francine rose like a puff of yeast.

"And I must get to work. Nice to see you both again." I balanced my hand on the table and stood to put on my coat.

"Too bad. I would have enjoyed some company this morning, but alas . . ." Didier made a scattering gesture with his hand.

"No worries, *chéri*, I'll bring you your usual and you can relax here with your bad news." Francine winced at the newspaper. "I never read them anymore." She waved good-bye and floated off behind the counter.

"Well, bad news is part of life! Who wants good news all the time?" Didier looked at me as if stating the obvious.

"I completely agree." I swooped up my things. "Have a good day, Didier. Not *too* good, of course . . ."

Didier smiled and sweet creases enfolded around his mouth like one of his wife's tempting elephant ears.

I left the café feeling like I'd forgotten something. A missing thought or gesture. This feeling of loss was happening a lot lately, a sudden off-balance moment like some critical thing had diminished so much in importance that it became no longer visible, no longer recognizable. With nothing to keep me from returning inside, I found my way to my car. As I passed the rusted gas station and the corner doughnut shop with its coffee-to-go sign, the spell was broken. No longer in the discreet charm of the sixth arrondissement, I secretly wished for Café Antoinette's survival and my own.

CHAPTER 8

THE YOUNG COUPLE LOCKED hands as they meandered across the large green campus, alternately looking up at the sun, then down at their shadows on the pavement, as swinging arms formed an outline of their spirited union. They glanced at one another with fast, instant smiles, perhaps imagining a piece of life together longer than the day, the moment, imagining themselves capable of more than shadows and squints.

I watched them drift past, thinking them naive as they cast their fate in the sunlight. I could recall feeling that vulnerable and shiny. The memory made my skin chill. The past tense of it. Young love was such a torturous, fleeting affair. Having time, stability, loyalty—these things were more important, more precious. At least, one had to believe they were.

I plucked a dead leaf off my desk plant, reminding myself that spring was dangerous. This annual reawakening, this hormonal pulse.

Everything bristling with hothouse potential. The forceful thrust of it was visible everywhere. I could smell its sensuality in the campus halls, feel it creeping up my bare neck as I lectured on the *accent aigu* and the use of the *cédille*.

"*C'est un garçon bien aimé*," I said to illustrate my point. *He is a well-liked boy.* Or "*La satisfaction instanée n'est qu'une façade.*" *Instant gratification is just a façade.*

The students seemed to melt into the language more in the springtime, savor it more profoundly. They even requested that class be held outdoors, picnic-style, on Fridays under the large oak, coming to class with baguettes and cheese for everyone to sample as they sprawled out on the lawn. I indulged them, hoping it would create more connection to the language, knowing full well that the only way to accomplish true fluency was to either move to France or take on a French lover, the same as I had done.

My two-year postgraduate work-stay in France had ended with me falling in love with the country. Immediately upon my return to New York, I fell for Martin too. He was the only vestige of Gallic representation I could find in lower Manhattan. He lived off scraps in the city and returned to Paris every few months to renew his tourist visa and pull together enough money to return to the States as quickly as possible. He stayed on people's couches and walked their dogs to earn his keep. He slept all day and soaked up the jazz scene at night, looking for impromptu jam sessions where he could play sax or learn some new riffs from more seasoned musicians.

We met on a street corner where he was playing for tips, a well-worn brown felt hat placed dutifully on the dirty city ground. His English was poor and he was poorer. And though his playing wasn't very sophisticated either, he was clearly elevated by the music. It was a fervor I'd rarely seen except in the company of certain artists and intellectuals. He was my imaginary path back to France. Back to the land of aloof stares, disinterested party chatter, and cigarettes. Somehow, some way, I felt coveted around those things.

A rare fluency in my tongue and a visceral appreciation for the French, I was invited in, an American oddity. They let me stay. And I wanted to be there, to remain a hidden treasure in all the wreckage. To shine because of my difference. To smile more than I ever intended. To breathe more foul tobacco-tainted air and leftist opinion than I could muster. It was a test of my will for two beautiful years, and by sheer intention and focus, I did it. I became other. I would never blend in completely: my self-consciousness gave me away. But I shifted identities until my character was no longer the scrawny outline of a young girl from southern Connecticut, but rather a more expansive silhouette. I was bilingual and bi-continental and postdoctoral. This was larger than I'd ever been.

And there, looking completely satisfied with his lack of ambition and the sheer beauty of the moment, was Martin. I noticed the accent immediately as he spoke to the small crowd. We caught eyes and I answered him back in French. The words caught him like a lasso and we spent the rest of the evening together discussing the history of Jews in jazz and the mistresses of Mitterrand. Our love affair lasted two months; by the third month I realized I was pregnant with Jacqui, and Martin wasn't feeling as free and easy anymore.

He was incapable of changing his life for the sake of a baby. I was incapable of giving up the chance of a child. I embraced motherhood, alone and defiant and unsure. Love, life, parenting—these were ambivalent roles in life. I never thought that having a man around would alter that ambiguity, just keep it company.

Martin and I parted ways, but remained linked to each other's lives. He became the close friend, the generous uncle, the quick visitor with a light heart and a small gift. Too broke to offer child support, too self-involved to sacrifice his own needs, too wannabe-Buddhist to claim any real attachments, Martin did the best he could, and I demanded nothing more of him. I was free to do with my life and my child whatever I desired. In the end, Martin gave me the ultimate connection to France: a daughter whose generous, paternal grandparents lived in Provence and relished long summers with their grandchild. My annual trips there with Jacqui were my consolation prize and my chief salvation.

Because of my history with Martin, I secretly wanted to impart to my students that fiery, passionate affairs with the French were the only ticket to fluency, and that all other efforts were futile. Intimacy with people and culture would be the only workable curriculum. But I also wanted to keep my job.

I settled for brief forays outside the language department with American-made attempts at French breads and cheeses and enjoyed them as much as the students did. It was a chance to break away from all the paths and patterns that constructed my life like a double helix inside me—rising every morning at the same minute and finding my way through the small, lifesaving gestures of making beds and preparing breakfast, readying for school drop-off and for work. I knew that one veering away from the daily script—one divergent action—and my life and its structure might collapse upon me. It made me want to chop off my hair, take kickboxing classes, and drive a Vespa to work.

Instead, I sat pruning the final yellowed leaf from my African violet, too fearful of an altercation with my psyche, and unable to bear the sight of things withering on the vine.

A jolting and unexpected knock came at my office door.

"*Entrez!*"

Didier Clébert stood there looking as sharp as an *accent aigu*. He combed his loose hair back with the palm of one hand and held out a maroon dossier with the other.

"You forgot this at the café this morning. I thought it might be important." He placed the file on my desk and smiled like a delivery boy about to get a raise.

"My papers? I can't believe I forgot them." But something in me *could* believe it; after all, I had gone to the café on a whim. It was not part of my usual routine. "You know, I had the distinct feeling that I'd left something behind this morning."

"I know what you mean." A pallor of nostalgia in his voice.

"Thank you, Didier, but you didn't have to bring the file all the way here."

"I know. But I had free time and I enjoyed the ride. It's nice countryside out this way. Perfect for the motorcycle."

"Motorcycle? Really?" Consensus on the Vespa. For a moment, this man seemed like an exotic nightshade growing wild in the sunny confines of Westchester. "Well, I appreciate the delivery."

"In fact, my motives were also a bit selfish." He stared pleasantly.

"Oh?" A self-conscious blush hung at the top of my cheekbones, ready to charge downward.

"Yes, I heard the university has an interesting art collection. Maybe I could have a look?"

My color regained, sudden composure trumping a gratuitous but real disappointment. "Of course! I'd be happy to show you where the museum is. It's a very small collection, but a nice one. All modern pieces, mostly abstracts. There's a recently acquired Calder in the main lobby. It's a big deal around here." I stood and put on my sweater, speaking a little too quickly, my pace accelerated. "Come, I'll take you there now."

We made our way over, stopping at the entrance of the large gray, rectangular building with colored glass windows and a piece of twisted metal art out front, signaling the destination as either an art museum or a recycling center.

"This is it. You'll have to let me know what you think."

Didier delivered a requisite light kiss to each of my cheeks. I again took in the lemony scent of him mixed with the sharp leather of his biking jacket. Then I headed back toward my office, examining the newly sprouted daffodils and crocuses, and the startling bursts of spring's surprise returns.

CHAPTER 9

"It's your ex." Along with the telephone, Dalton handed me a look of forced irony tinged with disgust.

I wanted to protest. The term *ex* was ridiculous. I was friends with Martin. Dalton insisted that calling Martin a *friend* concealed some truth about sex. The truth was that it irked Dalton endlessly that I had gotten pregnant so easily with this other man.

"*Allô . . .*" I took the receiver into the bedroom and began speaking French. It was as good as shutting the door on Dalton.

"That husband of yours really doesn't like me." Martin seemed to be smiling under his words. "What have I done? I just want to spend more time with Jacqui. Is this so terrible? So impossible?"

"No, it's not terrible at all. It's just that she has a really busy schedule. And finding time to get her into the city and back takes away from our family weekends." I tried to sound impartial, knowing how much Dalton hated the idea of Jacqui spending more time with Martin.

"Sorry, I don't have a car or I would come pick her up."

"Well, you could take the train and do something around here."

"And what? Sit in a café the whole day, staring at rich people? No, the idea is to show Jacqui the museums, the parks, real life in the city. All that."

"Why the to-do list all of a sudden, Martin?"

"Jacqui's got this wonderful perspective on everything. It excites me to be with her."

"But she's always been this way."

"Perhaps, but before, she was too young. A nine-year-old, I can relate to. Now we can really discuss things. I can expose her to art and music, and she responds so purely."

Martin had found a playmate. Someone his emotional age. Still, I found it hard to begrudge him time with his daughter. And wanting to enrich Jacqui with the wonders of city life was a tempting offer, and not something that Dalton or I could do so easily. "We'll figure out something."

"Meet me and we'll talk about it, okay? Come to Manhattan. Leave Dalton with Jacqui for an evening and just come. I want to spend some time with you too."

I could hear Martin chewing his nails, spitting out a tiny piece and making a small sound that I recognized from years of knowing his habits.

"I don't know why that husband of yours detests me. He should be grateful I gave him such a beautiful daughter, no?"

CAFÉ ANTOINETTE

"He is grateful. And he doesn't detest you." I heard the lie in my voice as clearly as Martin did. "Does next Thursday work for you?"

"Perfect. Meet me at Lincoln Plaza. Seven PM. There's a Polish film playing that we must see. We'll have some dinner and talk. Like old times, eh?"

"Only if you do all the talking." I hung up the phone, relishing the idea of a night out with my friend.

CHAPTER 10

I LOOKED FOR A CRUCIFIX TO string around my neck that night. Something to signal forbearance. But I could only locate a small, engraved locket with no one's picture in it. Better to go unloaded. Martin always tested me, pushed buttons, thrived on conjecture, debate. That night would be no different. I twiddled the empty heart between my fingers, steadying my pulse before the heady onslaught. Then I left for the city.

The last movie credit rolled off the screen and everyone remained seated, still needing time to privately relive something. It was a postwar story of lost love that seemed to make every moviegoer walk out reflecting on their own sorry amorous past. I could have lingered in the darkness for hours, but Martin was already up, stretching and nudging at me to move.

"I thought Roman was disgusting. I don't understand how she could love him."

"Are you kidding? He was perfect for her. She was miserable in her life; he was a great escape, the opposite of everything she ever knew. Okay, so he was grossly egotistical. But he had a heart."

"He was a jerk. He didn't deserve to be her first lover." Martin let the escalator deliver his scowl to street level.

"He was the right choice because he was passionate. She needed his passion to get out of her oppressive life. You just don't understand women." I forced a cool tone in my voice, the way French women do when stating the obvious or making announcements.

"*Moi?*" Martin shoved his fedora to the back of his head. "I understand women perfectly well! I treat women the same way I treat my saxophone: with love, respect, and tremendous care. It's a soft touch and deep understanding that matter most. I love to hear how they express themselves at different moments—sometimes humming, sometimes shouting. It's all poetry to my ears."

"Really? Interesting comparison. A woman is like an instrument you play and control." I picked up my pace as we entered the spotlight glare of Columbus Avenue.

"That is not what I meant!"

It seemed like we always disagreed. Martin was so fiercely dogmatic in his point of view. He saw debate as a joyful expression of opinion. He hated that Americans never perceived it that way, always laced with passive-aggressive gestures and competitive sneers. He would say, "If you're not opinionated, then what are you? Empty-headed?" For him, to be human was to have an opinion. A strong one.

We landed at a modest but hip bar that served good pizza. It was low-lit and well trampled. A quartet was warming up at the far end of the room. Soon it would be impossible to speak. Music would fill the empty pickup lines and holes in conversation, correcting all impaired senses. The first notes on the piano trickled randomly into space. The sax followed a scale and ended in the ethers. The cymbal hissed clean tin, abruptly muted by the drummer's deft hand. The bass slid up and down its lower register, tightening, loosening, until its heartbeat was steady.

Those in wishful conversation stayed their course, locking eyes with prospective partners. The rest let their attention shift to the musical core suddenly bursting forth with a flitty, aerial launch of *A Love Supreme*.

Martin let the tune instantly wrap him up in its four-note motif and turn his breath to heat. "Nothing like live jazz, eh?" The question was rhetorical.

We consulted the menu for a few seconds before Martin hailed down a waiter and ordered for both of us. It was an old habit he'd kept. He knew how to navigate my tastes. When he remembered the hot peppers and onions, I felt protected. Long ago, he had learned by heart every one of my likes and dislikes, as if committing to memory a series of Wayne Shorter riffs. But for some reason, there were many things I couldn't remember about Martin. We ordered a carafe of the house wine and I hoped a bit of recall would seep back with it.

"What was it like the first time you had sex?" Martin aimed his wineglass at me like a gavel.

"Me? Oh, I don't know. I can't really remember much about it at all. It was just a rite of passage. No real details, except that I was just lying there like an inanimate object. It was something that happened to me. I didn't really participate that much. At least, I don't think so."

I took a brave swallow of Chianti to wash down the vague apparitions of being unable to move in the backseat of a car. Privately, I was shocked not to remember what this first sexual encounter was like, what kind of car it was, what month it happened, or exactly how old I was. Sixteen? Seventeen? Wasn't that what the film was about—remembering the first time, savoring it, keeping a sacred piece of it with you your whole life? I lost my sacred piece. Another empty locket.

"Well, I remember every last detail. I will never forget it. Her name was Germaine. It was during our summer in Brittany. Like a fairy tale. It would make a very good film!"

"Of course it would, Martin. It's starring you!"

"Not me, but my life. You must remember these important times so you can share them with Jacqui at the right moment." He tore off the end of a roll and chewed on it. "Sourdough. I love sourdough."

"Hmmmm." My voice leaned into sarcasm. "I never considered telling Jacqui about my first time having sex. Or how bad it was."

"Ahhh, but you should! How else will she know what *not* to do? I will speak to her about my own beautiful story and you will tell her your foul, forgettable tale. Then she will know that the first time is important, and worth holding out for the right moment with the right person."

"Germaine."

"*Oui*, Germaine."

"Are you still in touch?"

"What? And ruin a perfect memory? No way." He took a reflective sip. "Anyway, she's probably quite fat, dripping in gold and talking too much now."

"Just like a saxophone." I smiled and took a long draw on my wine.

Martin toasted old times, wearing a big, extended grin on his face. No doubt thinking about Germaine. I clinked my glass to his. To the old times, the ex times, to us. Friends.

He pointed across the street to Lincoln Center, its fountain shooting up jets of illuminated water as sated patrons strolled out from an evening of high art, pausing in front of the grand Matisse tapestry to admire its beauty.

"I never told you, but I tried to get into Julliard."

"You did?"

"I tried. But I didn't make it." He shrugged and his tropical shirt quivered.

I never liked Martin's taste in shirts. Films, yes; shirts no. "So why didn't you ever tell me about it?"

"Why? Because I was too ashamed. There you were, this beautiful, intelligent woman with a PhD and already an associate professor at a university. And what? I taught myself to play the sax and Julliard thought I was terrible at it? How impressive, no?"

"Martin, you don't need Julliard to validate what a talented musician you are. And I was already very impressed by you."

"You were not impressed. Swept off your feet, perhaps. But not impressed. You were and still are an intellectual snob. And Julliard was right. Being told you're terrible when it's the truth is not such a bad thing. It meant that I had to go and work in my father's restaurant, which was torture for me. But it was also motivation to get better. Now I'm finally good at playing and Julliard can go fuck themselves."

Martin held his middle finger to the windowpane just as an innocent elderly couple walked by, no doubt assuming the gesture was meant for them.

"And us snobs, shall we go fuck ourselves as well?"

"Luci, please . . . it suits you. Academia, a fine life in the suburbs, a fancy, conservative husband . . ." He popped a caper in his mouth and seemed to enjoy souring a memory.

"Is that all you see? A typical bourgeoise?" I wanted to refute his accusation, his acerbic judgment, but something stopped me: The fact that maybe his memory was better than mine or that his notion was not completely wrong.

"What I mean is—"

I held up my hand to prevent him from apologizing. "I heard that being told you're something terrible when it's the truth is not such a bad thing."

His eyes filled with something I remembered. A sudden squint, a subtle shift to three-quarter view as if seeing me for the first time. Martin reached over and touched my hand. "There is nothing terrible about you or your life. What you've done is admirable."

"Even the fancy, conservative husband?"

"Well, him I can't be sure. But your kid is amazing."

"And you thought Roman was egotistical?"

Just then, the door of the restaurant flew open and a gaggle of midtown financiers paraded in. Martin's expression turned to disgust.

"Speaking of fancy and conservative, these people think corner cafés and live music will save them, make them human again. They're wrong."

"Oh, I don't know. I believe pizza and jazz can salvage even the most soulless among us."

"You think? Look at them! All in their twenties and making more money than you and I could ever imagine. I pity them their material world."

As they jockeyed for seats among the proletariat, fancy suit jackets dangled on bar stools like empty reminders of status—egos deflated for one happy hour or two. Ties loosened as the place filled and the temperature climbed. Sleeves got pushed up to better grab at pints and prospects. Entitlement echoed around us with youthful disregard. My eating pace slowed. Martin left all the crust on his dish. The carafe was finished. The music dipped to a jazzy lull: "Moonlight in Vermont."

Martin looked at me with something that resembled regret. We both knew why we had made certain choices in our lives.

"So, can I have Jacqui this weekend?" His voice almost sounded desperate.

"Sure." I'd explain it to Dalton later.

A light rain began to fall like in the final scene of a broken love story in some film.

"I should go before it downpours." I stood, ready to pay the bill and stop the stream of thoughts, grievances, confidences from issuing from my mouth.

Martin clasped his hand on top of mine. "Let me invite you this time."

As I stood in the rain out on the sidewalk, I imagined being permanently washed away, floating down the diagonal swathe of Broadway, pelted by raindrops and memories and deposited somewhere in the East River, peacefully adrift. For a moment, it held an appeal.

Martin looked back toward the music, as if taking a last glance at an alluring woman, then gallantly escorted me under his small, broken umbrella to the cab.

"I almost forgot. *Tiens*. A little something for you." He reached in his pocket and retrieved a small book with Buddha on the cover. "It helps me look at life and to remember the good things."

"Martin, you showed me this book when we first met."

"Ah, you see! It's working already! You remember!"

I remembered. His faltering, incomplete grasp of Zen. His sincere urge to understand, to follow.

"Well, now it's for you. And maybe one day for Jacqui. I have all the information I need right here." He tapped lightly on his temple.

"Right. Thanks." I squeezed his hand and got into the taxi holding the well-worn book in my palm. The cab sped away and Martin became a fleck on the shimmering avenue, tropical shirt waving in the wind and rain like a mirage blown away by a storm.

I looked down, comforted by Buddha's sudden company in the place of the missing martyr around my neck—happy to find a memory where one was once lost.

CHAPTER 11

JACQUI AND I TOOK THE TRAIN to Grand Central that Saturday after breakfast. She fidgeted in her seat, lightly bouncing and humming the whole ride. Since the train was practically empty, I didn't stop her. She'd have the rest of her life to feel self-conscious and under control. This was a moment to let go, urges unchecked. I wondered what my own would be if I didn't have them so battened down. Maybe take off my shoes, sprawl across the bench and sing a favorite song as I watched the world in stutter frames out the grimy window.

Dalton hung back at home to play a round of golf. Someone else ran his store on Saturdays so that the family could spend time together. But once I told him that Jacqui was spending the weekend with Martin, Dalton was quick to make plans for himself. It didn't bother me. I would have some time without ritual. Some time to do something or nothing at all. I hadn't yet decided.

Jacqui ran into Martin's arms at the terminal like a scene I'd witnessed a hundred times. I knew that Martin's heart did its own waltz jump whenever she greeted him this way.

"*Voici ma petite fille!* I'll have her safely back here tomorrow evening at six PM. *D'accord?*" Martin gently stroked Jacqui's hair as he spoke and I pitied him for not getting to exercise these small gestures more often. Jacqui curled into him like a cat.

"Have fun, you two. We'll call tonight to check in." I waved them off as they floated arm in arm through the terminal, under the protective gaze of lions and virgins and fish—a frozen zodiac of painted stars to guide the world-weary home again or offer escape to those more itinerant.

The next train for Scarsdale was leaving in ten minutes. I was considering a coffee to kill time when a small group of men caught my attention as they gathered under the clock. They huddled together with large plastic bags and shopping carts full of trash-picked things. They were homeless—or maybe Grand Central was, in fact, their home. In either case, they were taking advantage of Saturday's low gear and the station's generous acoustics.

One man with missing front teeth pulled out a harmonica, blowing a first note and holding it until all the others fell in line, C major buzzing through bruised lips like a balm. The men came to attention, inhaling as deeply as their street-warfare, damaged lungs would plunge. The injured looks on their faces fell away with a sudden peal of church voices that rose like dead ancestors into the air. It gave pause to anyone on the way to somewhere unholy. The spirited sight of New York's destitute—singing of grace, toils and snares, the Lord and his loyal wretches. A brotherhood lifted up the city's cupola and hung over us like a low-flung cloud from some inbound angel. Their harmonies soared, their broken smiles connecting with each lyric as if every word was written just for them.

When it was over, the small, unmoving crowd burst into applause and reached for wallets, while the frozen heavens shifted perspective above us. I found myself under the bull and crab constellations, dabbing at my eyes.

"*C'était sublime, n'est-ce pas?*"

Martin? I turned around and was face-to-face with another apparition.

"Didier? What are you doing here?" My voice sounded more suspect than pleased.

"I just arrived on the ten-thirty train."

"Me too. I was dropping off Jacqui with . . . with a friend. She's spending the weekend in the city. And you?"

"I just came to shoot some pictures."

"Well, you picked a beautiful day for it."

"I know. Besides, Saturdays are the busiest days at the café. For all the people with their croissants and coffees, it is their happy escape. For me, this is mine."

"Of course." A flapping from the schedule board skipping through departures and arrivals diverted my attention. "Well, it looks like my train is boarding."

"You're leaving? But you've just arrived."

"I really have nothing else to do in the city. I just came to drop my daughter."

"And Dalton is waiting for you at home, I suppose?" The way he said his name made it sound so unrecognizable.

I thought about Dalton playing golf with his buddies. I secretly hated the sport for its slowness, its clubbiness, and ultimately for its great gender rift. "No, he's out with friends."

"Well, if you like, you are welcome to join me. I am on an expedition to discover the center of the center of the universe."

"Sounds intriguing. Where exactly would that be?" I was ready for him to name a museum.

"Central Park. North meadow field. I saw it on a map." He was grinning like a child about to discover buried treasure.

"So, you actually mapped out the center of the city?"

"Not very precisely, but yes, I did. Most people would think that midtown is the center, but it's not."

"It's a field."

"Exactly. And I wish to see what it's like to be in the center of the center of the universe and who else will be there."

"Probably children. Playing ball."

"You never know. Your being here is already most interesting. The universe may be telling you to join me."

"Well, if the universe says so . . ."

I found myself on another train: the number one train heading north. My impulses became less obstructed with each stop. We got off at 110th Street and headed toward the park. North meadow was a huge stretch of ball fields, several acres long and across. Every inch of it filled with children in matching T-shirts, families with coolers, and coaches with whistles.

"So, this is the center of the center of the universe. Metaphorically speaking, of course." I waited for his response.

"Perfect, isn't it? Just as I had imagined, but so much better." Didier got his camera out of his bag and attached the right lens. "Everyone thinks about power brokers, fashion, art, and eight million people on the streets when they think of Manhattan. But at the heart of this place, it's not massive high-rises and thousands of taxis. It's open green fields, children and games. The center of the center of the universe is baseball—a worldwide sport only for Americans, and yet unifying in every way. A perfect metaphor, actually."

"Where high-stakes egotism meets the common man." My own definition.

"Precisely."

He was photographing already. Scenes from the epicenter. I sat on a bench and took in a game of tots playing T-ball, their parents urging them to run in the right direction. This is what I did every week with Jacqui at her skating and ballet and swimming practices: I watched, I cheered, I hoped she'd get it right. It's what all the good moms and dads of the world did. But not Didier.

He was not a father and didn't have to undergo the consumptive weekly spectator sports, the sideline chitchat with other dutiful parents, the missed meals and fast foods and rush-rush-rush of it all. We were professionals at rooting on our prodigy and believing ourselves the better for it. Though most times, I sat hungry and unconvinced.

A four-year-old girl took a swing, making the ball pop up over her head and roll behind her. It should have been a foul, but before the referee could make the call, the child was tearing toward first base, clutching her helmet to her head, brown curls popping out along the edges. She couldn't decipher what everyone was yelling or that her parents were making a circular gesture with their arms, trying to get her to turn back around. The helmet blocked all sound, all sight. The only thing that this small girl knew as she rounded first was that she'd hit the ball. She was pure smiles and sweaty accomplishment as her dusty little feet landed on the soft base.

It pained me to see her expression turn to confusion as the umpire-dad lead her back to home plate, trying to explain that her ball was foul and didn't count, but that she'd have some more tries. For her, the whole point of the game was to hit the ball, and she'd done that successfully. What was all this fuss about?

I understood. I'd taken my best shot at a few things that never got off the ground, or had popped up so far over my head they left me wondering where they'd gone. Like getting tenured at the university or trying to have a baby with Dalton. After each attempt, I'd get back up, holding my breath, more focused and uncertain of what I was doing.

I turned and looked for Didier. He was snapping away, completely unnoticed by all the doting parents—the same parents who probably wouldn't sign a consent form to have their child's picture used for the league's promotional materials, but who were blind to the swarthy foreign man in the outfield shooting reams of images of their off-spring for personal use. This is what war photographers did: They blended into the background so that others wouldn't notice them or try to kill them. Didier was still alive and unquestioned by the gruff-looking dads, faces pushed up to the fence, thick fingers laced in between the chain link.

He jogged in from the field, casting off his cloak of invisibility with a huge grin on his face and moisture accumulating across his brow. "This voyage to the center of the center of the universe has made me very hungry. Want to get some lunch?"

"As long as it's not hot dogs and Cracker Jack."

We settled at the Boathouse Café in a shady spot outside. A sweet breeze came from across the lake while people enjoyed paddling in rowboats or exploring in gondolas. Sipping at white wine over a shared seafood platter, I felt thousands of miles away: Southern France, to be exact. Dalton could have his golf games. This was a true escape.

"Tell me if you need to get back. I don't mean to steal your whole day." Didier relaxed back into his chair and a sliver of sun hit him on the side of the face, outlining it with yellow light.

"Actually, I'm fine. And no one is looking for me—quite a rarity." I checked my cell phone and held its dull screen up as proof.

"In that case, I have one more indulgence that I'd like to do, if you agree."

"What might that be?" My head was already swimming with wine and my body overly sated from lunch. I had only enough room for one more forbidden thought and I tried hard to push it away, but it kept reflecting back at me, along with Didier's face in the sun.

"Come." He stood up, holding out his hand, perhaps anticipating my wobbliness, perhaps out of gallantry. He led me to the edge of the lake where a vendor was renting boats and chose a canoe, which greatly relieved me as I did not find it at all desirable to pedal around in a paddleboat with my knees rising up to my chest on every downward push.

Didier helped me into the boat and I sat on the small wooden plank in the back as he took hold of the oars. The café din moved farther off, the sound of moving water and floating, idle conversation from not too distant boaters drifted in and out. I closed my eyes and gave thanks to the homeless men of Grand Central Station who had distracted me that morning, and in that pause issued an unexpected day of pleasure with not a speck of routine. That indeed was amazing grace. My eyes opened.

"Enjoying yourself?" He had caught me in my moment of quiet swoon.

I straightened, about to say *yes*, to say thank you for everything that he had done, for taking me along to his voyage to the center of the center of the universe and its surrounding areas. But then I saw something in the canoe behind us that took my breath away. A young couple, their boat tucked neatly in the tall reeds, thinking themselves invisible, their passion too great to hide.

The man was completely naked, his shirt and pants removed, his long, dark hair and tawny skin glinting from effort. She was not in view. Just pieces of her pale leg lifting up, her arms tightly gripping the sides of the boat for stability. He thrust inside her, his musculature alone an admirable sight. I couldn't take my eyes away from him. Didier quickly followed my gaze.

"Unbelievable . . ." His eyes lit up. Instead of rowing away from the scene, he took up his camera and began clicking off photos. Once again a warrior, indiscernible, inculpable, free.

"Didier . . . what are you doing?" It came out as a whisper, more sultry than I had intended, like something uttered in a moment of foreplay.

"*C'est beau,*" was all he muttered back, enraptured.

He was right. It was beautiful.

I didn't know who had less sense: the publically fornicating couple or the photographer capturing their intimacy. I wished for that kind of passionate, inconvenient lovemaking in my life. Something natural and spontaneous. But I also wished I could view the world with a different lens and not care so much how I appeared in its aperture. I wanted to disappear a little more. Something that I, a rather small-boned woman, could not accomplish, but that a tall, striking Frenchman with a large camera around his neck could.

Didier looked as captivated as the lovers while he photographed. I was the voyeur taking it all in: both his delight and theirs. I suddenly felt a surge of my own boldness, as if my shoes were finally off and I was sprawled out in a train and headed somewhere far, far away.

After another minute or so observing, we paddled away, naughty smiles on our faces.

"You know most people hide while they're having sex in public places. Tuck under the bleachers, shield themselves with beach blankets, the usual." I tried to sound knowledgeable.

"But why hide it? What they've done is so natural. There's no shame to it. It's pure expression. Pure attraction." His eyes seared into mine.

A light sweat broke out on my body. "It's getting late. I should get home."

"I'll row us back." He rowed, muscles tightening with exertion, a gentle whistle emanating from his lips.

Those lips. There they were again.

That evening, Dalton asked what I'd done that day.

"Same old, same old," was all I could muster.

I couldn't tell him that I'd voyaged to the center of the center of the universe and that it was baseball fields and open-air sex. Dalton's camera held a still life, not a *tableau vivant*. It was clear to me from that day forward that the unmentioned would insidiously tuck itself between our seemingly open exchanges. The missing words and feelings would be blatantly there, but if ignored, become as undetectable as lovers in a canoe hiding between the reeds.

CHAPTER 12

"Don't you just love the names on these things?" Sabine picked up a bottle of polish and turned it upside-down. "'Crush on You'. That's what I'm going for. That or 'Lola-Licious'. Either way, I want red. You?"

The display rack spun slowly. I checked for a color with some vamp to it. "Here it is: 'Key West Sunset'."

"Nice. Shall we?" Sabine led the way to the large black leather massage chairs where the pedicurists were waiting to help us off with our shoes and seat us in vibrating seats.

"Your friend, she like it deep, like you?" The young Korean woman glanced knowingly at Sabine.

"I won't touch that one with a ten-foot pole." Sabine smiled back politely.

The robotic gears were churning, digging into the tender parts of my lower back while my feet soaked happily in the vortex of the

Jacuzzi's hot, bubbly water. "This is my first pedicure of the season. I forgot what a treat it is."

"Not me. I do them all year long. I want my feet looking good."

The pedicurist laughed. "Your feet always look good, Sabine. I make sure of it. Can I offer you and your nice friend some tea?"

"No thanks, Lina. This time, I brought my own drink." Sabine reached into her leather bag and pulled out a bottle of Moët & Chandon. "Got glasses?"

Lina clapped her hands and yelled something in Korean to the rest of the salon workers. The other manicurists raised their unpolished hands in a mock toast.

"Are we celebrating something today?" I wondered if I had missed some important occasion.

"Just life. We are celebrating life. Today makes two years that I had my double mastectomy." She gave her implants a celebratory squeeze. "I've been cancer-free for two years. Can you believe it?" Her face flushed and her eyes blinked away any doubts.

"Now that's really something to celebrate! Congratulations, girlfriend!"

The glasses arrived and Lina poured a little bit in each of them. Sabine raised her cup. "May I live to one hundred and keep the rest of my body parts!"

Lina squawked with laughter, drinking to Sabine's long life and happiness. We sank an inch deeper into our chairs and let the effects of the tingling wine and hot water work their magic.

"How often do you have to check in with your oncologist?"

"I'm due for an appointment this month. God forbid she finds anything, I'll put a bullet in my head."

"Sabine! Why would you even think that? You're fine. Besides, you're a fighter. Fighters don't give up."

"Believe me, I've hung up my gloves on this one. After getting through the first round, losing my breasts, my hair . . . I even lost my husband, for Christ's sake! I still can't believe we divorced in the middle of all that. Can you imagine? He was the real cancer in my life. But to go through it all again . . . I couldn't. The first time you fight because you have to. You don't know any better. But once you've seen the war and lived it, you have the right to wave a white flag. Believe me."

"Well, you won't have to."

Sabine raised her glass as her free hand slid down her shapely frame. "But hey, look at me. I made the most of it: breast implants, tummy tuck, face-lift—the whole nine yards. That divorce settlement got me a new lease on life." A satisfied look washed over her taut expression as she contemplated the medical miracles of her existence.

"I think I need one of those." My voice trembled as the chair pounded my lumbar.

"Which one: the plastics, the divorce, or the new lease on life?"

"The new lease. Definitely."

"What's going on?"

"I don't know. Everything is status quo, but I feel something shifting in me. I don't know what it is."

"You're waking up. Status quo sucks." Sabine placed her leg outside the footbath and waited for her calf rub to begin.

I leaned in so as not to be overheard by Lina. "I'm having fantasies."

"*Oooh.* Good for you!"

"Yeah, but these are about someone who's married!"

"Doll, you're fantasizing because Dalton does nothing to intrigue you. It's the same old tricks with him. Lots of women have to live with their husbands' plain vanilla routines. The key is to spice it up for ourselves in other ways. Fantasies are the easiest way. And harmless too. I say, go for it."

"It doesn't feel harmless. It feels obsessive."

"So it's a crush. 'Crush on You'. Just like the bottle says. Who's the guy? A professor?" A mock-scandalous look on her face.

"No. Nothing like that. He's . . . he's my secret Belmondo. That's who he is."

"French. Figures. You're hopeless, you know that?"

It felt good to tell someone. Someone who wouldn't judge me or ask too many questions. My glass refilled with another round. I relaxed into the gyrating seat, hoping that the vampy color being applied to my toes wouldn't give my lust away.

The chime rang at the front of the salon signaling the arrival of a new customer. A faint silhouette entered, followed by the usual flurry of nods and greetings from the manicurists. I paid no attention to the newcomer and surrendered to my foot rub with thoughts of Frenchmen floating in my head.

"*Salut, Luci.*"

I looked up. There was her outline, barging in on my confession, jolting me from my reverie, like a jealous wife confronting the adulterous mistress.

"Francine?"

"*Que le monde est petit . . .*"

"Yes, indeed." The world was feeling too small at the moment.

I shut off the chair, probing my spine and jiggling my midsection to embarrassing effect, and tried to regain composure. "Francine, I'd like to introduce you to my dear friend, Sabine Lowenfeld."

Sabine's chair continued to whiz and whir and make its therapeutic assault, her large implants remarkably unshaken. She barely opened her eyes, but raised a hand to say hello.

"Nice to meet you, Francine. This place is the best, isn't it? Would you like some champagne?"

"Champagne? Obviously you get better treatment here than I! Thank you, but no. I just came for a quick manicure."

"Sorry, Miss Francine, but you'll have to wait a few minutes. You can wait here." Lina patted the seat next to mine, inviting Francine to sit. Francine folded into it, tapping her knees as if keeping time.

"*Elle est jolie, cette couleur.*" Francine pointed to my toes.

"Oh, you like it? I'm trying something new."

"I never do anything so bold. Just pale pink all the time. It's easier for work." She uncrossed her hands and I wondered if Didier liked his wife's pale pink nails the way I liked Dalton's pinstriped suits. Hardly noticed for their rigorous dependability. If I knew Francine better or liked her husband less, I might have convinced her to go for a more expressive color. Something with sex appeal. But "Sunset in Key West" was my only advantage.

"Didier is really looking forward to his show. He's very excited to exhibit these photos. They mean so much to him." She had a maternal tone.

"So, the photographer coming to the French Club is your husband?" Sabine opened her eyes, getting the whole picture.

Francine nodded, inhaling a small *oui*.

"Well, I'll be there. I've heard some really nice things." Sabine's smile was omniscient.

"Yes, well . . . we're all looking forward to it."

Francine was suddenly waved over to an open chair, ready to paint her blunt nails an invisible, reliable pink. "Nice chatting with you ladies. Enjoy! *Chin-chin!*"

When Francine was out of earshot, Sabine looked over at me. "She better be careful. A marriage can't survive on 'Ballet Slippers' alone."

She spoke slyly and knowingly into her glass, and I raised mine in full agreement.

CHAPTER 13

The doors to the French Club opened at seven PM. Didier arrived a few hours before to help set the images up on easels and adjust the track lights on the ceiling.

"I apologize, but the lighting will never be perfect." It was my admission of guilt about such a mediocre setting for his fine art.

"I don't look for perfection. It's too much of a burden. The imperfect is fine with me. This is all just fine with me." He adjusted the final spotlight, singeing his fingers for a second before surrendering them to the balm of his tongue.

I tried not to stare at his mouth. "I'm glad you're pleased. I know everyone will love what they see tonight."

"Love it or not, I hope it makes them think. That's what matters. I don't care about giving them pleasure. I want to leave an impression on their memory, their consciousness."

An American artist might have said a simple "thank you." I had to remind myself of the particular manner that the French had of politicizing everything, theorizing everything. I looked up at Didier as he descended the ladder.

"Well, I can personally attest that I haven't forgotten any of these faces since the moment I first saw them." I considered his own to be among them.

He nodded, surveying the images around us. "I think your idea of making a ring with the photos around the room, around the people, is brilliant. I would have not thought to do it like this. It has more of an impact this way, like we're surrounded in some kind of ritual circle. Whether one of life or death, it's uncertain. I like the ambiguity." He folded his arms and turned slowly in the center of the space.

I stared at the young faces and they seemed to stare right back. The height of the easel also lent gravity to the photos, propped up to the stature of each child. A small, white card under the picture gave the child's name and age and a few lines of information about his or her brief existence. There was something deeply troubling and impossibly poetic in those few lines, as if a handful of words could ever surmise anyone's life.

The caterer showed up at six to set up the hors d'oeuvres and the wine. Dalton and Jacqui arrived soon after, followed by Sabine and Omar. Francine Clébert entered in a flurry, carrying two large boxes of petits fours, which she whisked off to the kitchen with a pleasant *"Salut, chéri,"* barely making eye contact with either her husband or his exhibit as she shuttled past.

As each person entered the room, a silence took them over at once, crushing small talk down to a whimper. The fuller the room got, the quieter it became. Like the very air was being squeezed out of it—a church congregation in a moment of solemn prayer, a town after an apocalypse. Everyone realized that they were as much on display as the photos. Their very humanity was on exhibit. I took Jacqui by the hand and we slowly clocked our way around the images, taking in each one, each face and name and detail.

Jacqui noticed the small things: the minor evidence of broken toys in the background, half of a word on a torn shirt, a fly perched on a knee. A sense of injustice was rising in her as she read about the lives, the deaths, the brutalities of war. This was a world she had never seen or heard of: A life away from parents, far from a clean, soft, safe place to lay one's head at night. This was a life where children bore arms, murdered neighbors, and carried dead siblings on their backs. After the fifth photo she stopped asking me why, letting go of my hand at one point and standing eye level with her dead peers from the Congo.

"Do you think she should really be seeing all this?" Dalton drew his eyes away from the photographs as if they were causing too great an offense.

"I do. This is important. I know it's hard, but she'll remember it. You should try looking at them too."

When Jacqui had made it round the room once, she turned back and started again. Though she could hardly lift her legs to take another step or revisit all the pained stories and beautiful faces, it became clear that the effort alone would make her stronger. Dalton followed.

Sabine found her way over to where I was standing. "Well, this stuff will make you count your blessings."

"I know. Isn't it amazing?"

"Yeah. And Belmondo isn't so bad himself . . ." A look of knowing drew itself across her face, invisible lines connecting her thoughts.

"Sabine! Shhh! He'll hear you!"

Sabine turned to see Omar chatting softly with Didier. "I wonder what those two are talking about? Shall we?"

We moved in closer to join them. Didier was holding court, too impassioned to notice our arrival.

"—and being on the ground in Congo was hard enough, but taking the pictures was troubling. The tricky part was trying not to objectify these children who had been objectified enough. They needed to be the subjects, the authors of their own portraits." Didier looked into Omar's large black eyes as if communicating religion to him.

Omar shook his head in sympathy and agreement, then asked if Didier would mind taking Sabine's portrait one day. Didier just smiled as if his very faith were broken.

My black, wool crepe dress swished against my stockings as the crowd gathered in the center of the room. People clustered together, barely enough appetite for all the little savory hors d'oeuvres being served. Every gesture felt somehow self-conscious, frivolous. It was, after all, bad taste to be eating surrounded by images of starving children. But this was New York, not the Congo, and irony was never lost on its citizens.

Didier took the floor to an extended round of applause. The sound barrier was finally broken, questions ensued, emotional discourse flowed, and eventually, appetite resumed. By the end of the night, when the last dozen petits fours lay idle on a silver tray and the children of the Congo returned to their big black box, it felt as if, for once, I had done something worthwhile, not just something cultural or gluttonous. But something memorable.

"Congratulations." I placed my hand on Didier's shoulder. "The evening was a resounding success."

His body was still kinetically charged from all the talk and praise, all the teary handshakes and searing compliments. Like he was on new ground. His eyes darted, his hand grabbed mine, wanting to give back some of what he was feeling, but not quite knowing how.

"Luci, I can't thank you enough. I wasn't expecting such a strong reaction. I thought—well, it doesn't matter what I thought. Tonight was wonderful. I found myself again. My art. My purpose. I'm very grateful to you."

My hand still lingered in his. "I did nothing. This is all because of you."

There was a sudden realization that we were still touching, then an instant releasing of hands, still fixed in each other's gaze. The ritual good-night pecks on the cheek landed with length and substance, not abandoned to the air. Like something extra and necessary was being communicated. The usual token embrace lasted a second or two longer. I could feel the strength of his arms under his jacket.

"Where is your family?" Didier searched the room for signs of their presence.

"Jacqui needed to get to bed. Dalton took her back."

"So, you're alone?"

Suddenly, the door popped open. Francine stood, keys dangling, rubbing at her temples with exaggerated effort.

"Ready, *chéri*? I'm exhausted and I have to wake up at four AM."

He disengaged. "Yes, of course. Ready."

The Cléberts left the building, Francine mildly complaining about the late hour, Didier still trying to hold onto the exultation of the evening, and me wondering what might have happened if his wife hadn't entered the room when she did.

CHAPTER 14

It wasn't just in the name of breakfast that Café Antoinette was becoming a regular stop for me. It was also to catch a moment with him, share a word, a look, to start my day with a feeling of desire. The rich, sweet aromas and smooth espresso were an added stimulation in a series of otherwise mundane routines. But seeing Didier was slowly becoming my nourishment.

As I headed in from the parking lot, his voice came from behind the service door. I took a few steps toward the entrance, about to signal hello when I noticed Francine shielding her eyes with one hand, her free arm wrapped tightly around her small waist as if holding herself up completely. Didier braced her with his grip, trying to drive her gaze toward his. I stepped back, not wanting to be seen, but too curious to walk away.

"—know how it is for me. I get crazy. I have to do this. It's what I do. You saw the reaction from the exhibit. I'm so out of my element here. It's too much."

"But you've been here less than a year, and we've been apart for so long. I think this will ruin us."

"Seriously? You would say that? Because I have done nothing but support you and your dreams since the very beginning. And me? I don't have the right to do my work and follow my own dreams? Really?"

"Didier, I don't mean it like that. But I don't know how much more I can take. I feel like you're always in some kind of competition with me, with my success. It's unreasonable." Her voice rose a pitch as she spoke, none of the usual sweetness to it.

"I'm competing with no one. Especially not with you. How can you think that? Are you so selfish? Don't you understand that I have my art, my career too? For the first time in years I feel like I have a purpose again. I'm going to take the assignment, Francine. I'm sorry if you don't agree. But I have to take it."

"No, you don't have to. You want to. Face it. You want to be as far away from me and this place as possible. I'm sorry I strangle all your artistic potential. I was just trying to build a comfortable life for us. But obviously, whatever I do is not enough."

The door sounded shut and the momentary silence made me jolt. I froze, not knowing in which direction to move. Footsteps came closer. Didier looked surprised to see me standing there.

"Luci?" His expression was confounded, undone.

"Hello, Didier. I just came for my morning jump-start." I tried to seem innocent.

"Yes. Well, sorry, I have to go." He headed off toward his car, his boots making loud crunching noises in the gravel like angry words issuing from under his breath.

"Okay. See you later." I stood there, heart thumping from my indiscretion, wondering about what I'd overheard, questioning if the show at the French Club had somehow plummeted him toward some kind of decision, and if my pleasurable stops at Café Antoinette would soon come to an end.

"Didier?" I called out to him before I could stop myself.

He turned, his thoughts still tangled in his wife's displeasure.

"Do you need to talk?" I tried to hide any sign of treachery in my voice.

He waved his hand as if to say *no*, then turned back. "Not here." He signaled me to get in his car.

I made my way to the passenger side of the vehicle and climbed in. As the car pulled out of the lot, I noticed someone looking at us from inside the café. Francine? I couldn't tell.

"I just want to drive around. Is that okay with you?"

"Sure, it's fine."

"Funny I should see you at this moment. You're probably the only person I can speak to in this town. It's not just a question of language, either."

"I'm happy to be here for you." I smiled, feeling a bit sick for spying on his affairs, then engaging his trust. I looked to the side rearview mirror, my hair tussled, my intentions blurred; I barely recognized myself.

"I got offered an assignment. A big one. In Africa again. This time following a peacekeeping unit. They bring clean water and infrastructure to the Sudanese refugees. It means time in Darfur and parts of Uganda. Two months, maybe more."

"Wow, Didier, that's incredible. Congratulations."

"You see? You're happy for me, no? It's normal. Francine, she doesn't want me to go."

"I'm sure she's just thinking about how much she'll miss you."

"Well, this is my work and I've always supported her work, without question or hesitation."

"I understand. Still, it must be challenging for her. That's a long time apart." A look of concern masked my own sense of loss in Francine's. "When would you be leaving?"

"At the end of June. First I'd go to France to prepare. Then, the Sudan." He coasted down the tree-lined streets, his breath short, anticipating some roadblock.

"It doesn't sound like you have any uncertainty about it."

"I do, of course. But this work defines me. I can't spend my life roaming the suburbs of Manhattan looking for interesting subjects. The exhibit—it convinced me of this. I need to get back out into the world and not keep showing the same images that I made so many years ago." His foot landed on the brake as he turned to face me. "You understand that, don't you?"

Most people would be happy to live off their laurels. Isn't that why people found me interesting—the time I spent in France in my twenties, the degrees I'd achieved since? Certainly, it was nothing in my recent history. I thought of Francine and her pastry awards, the ones listed on her menu. Sometimes people held onto old meanings because new ones were so scarce. But I wanted to be the compassionate counterpart to Francine—to be Didier's confidante, the supportive woman in coral varnish with empathy in her heart.

"I think you're very brave, Didier. Most of us will never even have the opportunity to do something new and exciting, face danger, tell meaningful stories. Never." My own life was a perfect example, with its dull schedules and lusterless duties. I longed for the shiny pull of other worlds. For the center of the center of my universe.

He nodded silently, considering my words. "I've been wanting to give you this." He reached into his bag and pulled out a large brown envelope. A photograph slid out from the inside. It took me off guard. It was a picture of me on the ball field, watching.

"I had no idea."

"You were so pensive. I tried to imagine what was making you so engrossed. Whatever it was made you a much more interesting subject than the children themselves. Hope you don't mind."

"Mind that you stole my soul without asking?" I suddenly felt naked.

"It's what I do. And this one is the best shot. Your expression is so incredible. So lost in thought. What were you thinking about, if I may ask?"

I paused, remembering. "I was thinking about rules."

"In baseball?" He squinted to understand.

"And in life. Like how a person can be happy thinking they're making all the right plays, until someone inevitably comes along and tells them what they're doing is wrong, and to play by the rules or leave. I hate rules."

"Yes." His stare caught mine and wouldn't let go. "I hate rules too."

I was suddenly uncertain of which set of laws we were referring to. But one thing was for sure: I would miss Didier Clébert and the wonderful distraction he gave me.

"Good luck with your trip, Didier. And thanks for this." The photo balanced in my hands like a mirror under me, showing a more reckless, rebel self. I could show it to no one. Because wandering around the city unchecked, intimately photographed by a handsome, married man was definitely not in the rule book.

Didier smiled at the far corners of his tentative mouth, his thoughts already accumulating, his days already gathering water near the Sudan.

CHAPTER 15

NORMA TENDED TO LAUGH louder whenever Dalton was in the room or telling a joke or commenting how Mondays were his favorite days because of the way the house gleamed. Dalton and his hygiene. Dalton and Norma, like a united front against dirt. I hated Mondays. Hating Mondays was a national pastime. No matter how much I enjoyed a sparkling kitchen and freshly folded linens, it was almost unpatriotic to love Mondays simply for the whitewash they created over the pleasures of the weekend. Mondays made me not want to cook or shower or get out of bed. They made me hungry for the grit of Friday.

Norma roared into the living room, vacuum blasting, head thrown back in a cackle from some charmed greeting Dalton gave her. "Mr. Dalton, you always put me in a nice mood."

Dalton, feeling like he had just done his good deed for the day, his gesture of routine kindness toward the working class, yelling "My pleasure!" over the roar of the Dyson. My thoughts were unwarranted. Still, I resented this Monday-morning confederacy of clean and left the bedclothes on the floor as a sign of my disapproval.

On Mondays I had advanced French conversation class, followed by my course on twentieth-century French culture and history. Then lunch with Sabine and a welcome respite of listening, instead of the day's required hours of lecture.

I descended the slippery hardwood stairs, thinking about the runner we never got, the need for tread to keep from sliding, Jacqui's numerous spills from wearing socks on the bare floor. There were so many small decisions that I put off, not wanting to invest in the permanence of this particular existence. A piece of carpet, a flagstone walkway, a patio deck. Dalton constantly urged me to make up my mind. Choose. But I never could. Imagining all this missing flooring often caused me to lose my balance. The indecisive, raw elements of our home would have to suffice. Especially on Mondays, when stasis was all I could bear.

Dalton stood leaning on the kitchen counter perusing the *Times*, cup of coffee in one hand, bagel in the other. Jacqui was finishing her cereal and watching the end of a cartoon program. Norma was practically dancing with the hose, causing static on the screen and a dull throb between my eyes.

"Norma? Do you mind waiting till we're done breakfast?" It was not the first time I'd asked this of her. For some reason, she always forgot. It seemed to me that perhaps a young, single woman like Norma craved early-morning moments with a husband and a child, indulging in routine domesticity under the gaze of all and no one. No wife in sight.

Norma quickly shut off the appliance and smiled. "Right. Sorry. I'll start upstairs." She took hold of her bucket and supplies and walked assuredly up the dubious slope of the stairwell to conquer dust and loneliness in the bedrooms.

"There's something different about Norma today." I poured myself half a cup of coffee.

"Is there?" Dalton finished off the last bit of bagel, wiping his mouth on a French-provincial print napkin and grabbing his things.

Poor Norma. All this exuberance for a man who didn't even notice.

"Jacqui, go brush your teeth and let's get going." I gave a gentle poke to the small of her back.

Jacqui dropped her bowl in the sink, flinching from the sound of ceramic against metal and lifting her eyebrows in a well-practiced gesture of apology.

"No four-dollar lattes this morning?" Dalton peered at me from over his paper.

"It's either espresso or cappuccino. Never latte. Too much milk. But no. Your world-famous, economical *jus de chausette* will do me just fine today." I glanced at my husband, his watery brown coffee, his telling brown eyes.

"Sock juice? That bad?"

I nodded and took another sip. "But I can weather even your worst cup of joe." I somehow wanted collusion with Dalton. I wanted to tell him not to worry, that Didier was leaving for Africa. That life would go on the way it was, privileged and listless and incomplete.

"That's my girl! Through better or worse . . ." He leaned over to kiss me good-bye, shouting his departure up the deadly stairs to Jacqui and Norma, who echoed back farewells.

I finished off the rest of the cup and gathered my things and my daughter. I'd return that evening to the gleam. The one in Dalton's eye as he entered his perfectly antiseptic home, the one in the freshly polished furniture and high-shine appliances. The blinding fake smile of Monday would assail me soon enough.

"Norma?"

"Yes, Miss Luci?" She appeared on the landing of the second floor like a fair young woman banished to the tower.

"You changed your hair. I like it. It looks really nice." My most sincere smile.

Norma blushed. "You think so?"

"I do."

"Me too!" Jacqui piped in. "You look like Princess Jasmine!"

The three of us laughed as Jacqui and I headed out the door to face the day and enter the secret union of damsels slipping from one disenchanted venture to the next, hoping to be saved.

CHAPTER 16

I ARRIVED ON CAMPUS AND parked in the same spot as usual—a numbered spot just for me. And because of the location of spot fifty-eight, I walked the same route to my office, never veering. I wondered if there was some deeper meaning to the number? Nineteen fifty-eight was the year my parents had met. I'd probably travelled to at least fifty-eight major cities across the world, though never took the time to count. Maybe I'd slept with fifty-eight men. Who could say for sure? And fifty-eight was also Sabine's age. And though fifty-eight was definitely something, it wasn't nearly enough.

I walked over to the far end of the lot to space number 116 and slipped a note on the windshield, asking the owner if they wished to switch spots with me. Either way, my parking days were numbered. The semester was ending and I'd have the length of the summer months ahead. Not quite 116 days, but good enough. Of course, part of it was taken up by the monthlong trip back to France with Jacqui. To the rest of the world, it seemed like a big, enviable getaway. To me, it was routine. But in this case, it was one that I cherished even if I always made it seem tedious to Dalton.

Maybe Dalton was making things he cherished seem tedious to me too. Like working late nights. Perhaps we were more the same than it appeared. After all, couples rubbed off on each other after a number of years, didn't they? I was certainly less freewheeling than before and fit better in social circumstances. I'd become more polished, homogenous. Some of Dalton's varnish must have smeared on me, taking the untamed right out.

This, I do for me. That was what I used to tell myself before jumping off a rocky coast in Croatia with only a full moon to guide me, or before engaging in a romantic tangle with a sun-basted traveler in some remote village. These were not escapades that I bragged about or gave much thought to. They were simply the moments that made up my life and allowed me to feel brave and autonomous and very unlike the budget-conscious American vagabonding across the globe looking for a greater purpose, or competing with blonder, more beautiful women from Nordic countries—topless creatures, from endless, leggy swathes of land that froze and burned at just the right times of year. Those were definitive women for whom it was all or nothing. Deep darkness or midnight sun. Jumping off low, foreign cliffs in war-torn countries during a lunar cycle made me almost feel analogous. Taller, in any case.

These days there was less rebellion to cling to. Just memory. My travels had taken me to a lot of places, all catalogued in my mind so that I could go back and relive portions of them in my sleep or while bored at my desk, pulling dead leaves off a plant I never wanted to care for—another live thing to keep me grounded when all I wanted was to pull up roots.

Certainly, home was not Wallingford, Connecticut where my parents still lived. Close enough to visit several times a year and far enough to keep separate lives. They never understood my love for France, and especially not for Martin. But their affection for Jacqui was indisputable. For Dalton as well, as if he were some debonair man in uniform who swooped in and plucked me out of oncoming traffic. My mother sided with Dalton on every matter, while Dad squinted with quiet judgment as if Dalton had injured him in some way by being more successful, more generous, better looking.

A knock came at my office door as I crumpled the remnants from my limp ficus. *"Entrez!"* I yelled, not bothering to ask who it was.

A tall, young Middle Eastern–looking man walked in holding a piece of paper and smiling wryly. "Dr. Ames?"

"Yes. Is there something I can I do for you?"

"I don't know. Maybe there's something I can do for you. I found this note on my car." He wore a pleasant look on his face as if he'd just won a wager.

And though the youthful teaching assistant thought that I was doing him a favor by casting my vote with numerology, I whispered to myself as he left my office: "This I do for me."

CHAPTER 17

BECAUSE PROFESSOR JAMES McCauley taught early European history and had a soft spot for royalism, he felt entitled to hold court wherever he went. He leaned into his colleague on line at the commissary and made his first decree of the day.

"All men watch porn, whether they admit to it or not. It's a fact." It sounded empirical when he said it.

The colleague—a lesser-degreed man from the computer science department—agreed, adding that his own wife still didn't have a clue. They laughed and ordered trans-fatty lunch specials, which no doubt kept them lubricated and paunchy, increasing the probability of their need for porn.

I couldn't imagine Dalton watching that stuff. But Professor McCauley went on to say that any man who didn't surely couldn't claim a sex drive. He was definitive, as if the two things were inherently linked. I thought his comment ridiculous, disgusting even. I'd never watched much porn. Never wanted to. It seemed misogynist and hollow and entirely unsexy. But now that my own fantasy life was starting to take shapes I had never imagined, I understood the impulse. It was almost as if I had erotica happening in my head all the time. The question was: Was it any different to watch a third-party rendering?

Sabine stood on line next to me, not listening, too involved in deciphering the day's specials.

"Sabine, can you recommend something?"

"For lunch?"

"No, to watch. A good porn flick," I said in a low, almost imperceptible voice. "Something that shows the real deal as opposed to a bunch of fake stuff."

"I wish I could seem shocked but the facelift won't let me." She laughed. "Doll, you're barking up the wrong tree. The last porno I saw was *Deep Throat*. But I can ask Omar and the boys. . . ."

"No. That's all right. It's probably a stupid idea anyway." I felt a blush creeping up my neck, about to make a beeline.

"Not at all. I'm impressed by your thinking. Trying to make it sizzle with hubby?"

"Trying." It was a lie. I wasn't sure if the X-rating would secure a better foothold for Dalton or kick open the door for Didier to strut in. Naked, of course, and strapped with a holster full of heated essential oils.

"You know, I once read that foot rubs are the key to a long and happy marriage. Dalton is into feet, right?" Sabine was finding this all too amusing.

"No. He just sells shoes. No foot fetish."

"Too bad."

"I know. He says the last thing he wants to do at the end of the day is look at feet. And besides, he claims that too many different kinds of fungus can occur between the toes."

"I guess sucking them isn't an option either, then." A raucous laugh rose to the surface.

"I don't know what I'm thinking, Sabine. I'm being ridiculous."

"Ridiculous is better than tedious."

I knew it wasn't about the odd positions or the props or the lusty backdrop. It was about, beyond all measure, being desired. Being looked at in that animal, insatiable way. Wasn't lovemaking supposed to be a sensory affair? Wasn't it relishing in the scent, taste, feel, and sight of the other? Even though my love life had become a thrill-less monogamy, I was beginning to feel that a bigger loss was at stake.

"Can I tell you something odd, Sabine?"

"Please, the more graphic the better."

"I splash my face ten times with warm water each night and every morning. Not nine, not eleven. Ten times."

"So, what are you getting at, sweetie? You like to be clean?" Sabine's voice tendered as one would do with an upset child or a hospice patient.

"Lately, while I'm washing up, I forget things."

"Like?" She reached for a dinner roll.

"For instance, the other day I forgot what my nose looked like. Honestly forgot. Is it flat or bulbous, big or small? Piglike or pointy? When I opened my eyes, it was a huge relief to know that my nose was rather normal."

"Nothing like those other noses you mentioned."

"It's not a joke. Don't you see? I'm forgetting who I am. I'm living in fantasy land, strapped to a million small routines and forgetting what's real." I truly wasn't sure which assailant was more dangerous: fantasy or reality.

"I have the opposite problem. I remember exactly what I look like and yet every time I see myself in the mirror, I have no clue who's looking back. Now, *that's* fantasy land." She took a healthy bite of salmon.

"Well, whoever it is you keep seeing in the mirror, she looks terrific."

"Yeah. Until the hair falls out, the skin goes slack, and the smell of everything makes me vomit."

"At least until then." I had to keep our thoughts from descending into something too truthful. I felt ashamed to be thinking about my sex life when my best friend was always facing the threat of reoccurring disease. "Thanks for listening."

"Can't always be of much help, but I'll always listen."

I stared at my plate, feeling as distilled and shallow as the water in my glass. Surely, these very frivolities were why Didier had to leave this place and go to Africa. How could he possibly care about the vanities and damages of Scarsdale when entire worlds were coming to an end? Given all accounts, I had a good life, a privileged life—one I should hold onto and not trade in for casual flights of the imagination.

Out of self-preservation, I looked across the commissary and shot a very disapproving glance over at Professor James McCauley, reproaching his edicts over porn and fatty potatoes. I banished them like bad thoughts and clung instead to the image of a moonlit night in a faraway place, and a young, rebel woman standing on a cliff, about to jump.

CHAPTER 18

He pulled me close to him and kissed me, his mouth opening, his hands grasping me around the waist, touching the bit of skin that became exposed in the rush of embrace. We swam in each other's tongues, heat rising around the neck and face, desire playing its usual burning chords. My fingers opened a space between my body and my clothes, prying away my belt buckle. He deftly tucked his hand inside, sliding it down to touch me there. I sucked in my stomach, an invitation, a *yes*. He had to force access a bit, the belt still holding its grip. A sound came from the hallway. He stalled, his hand resurfacing. I pretended not to miss him and his deeply anticipated touch. He detached, like nothing had almost happened, wiping the heat from his face.

"Maybe I can see you again this week?" He smoothed out his shirt, his excitement still visible in his pants, his eyes darting toward the noise in the hall.

"Of course." I wanted to guide his hand back down so he could feel what he had done to me. Was it the sudden shadow in the hall or simply prudence that had stopped him? "Didier . . ."

"Oui?"

The words *I want you* were ready to fall from my lips. Instead, nothing came out.

I awoke from my dream, heart racing, body covered in sweat. The clock read five AM. My sudden movement woke Dalton.

"Hon?"

"Sorry, babe. Go back to sleep." Falling back asleep would be impossible. Not after that. I lay in bed and tried to evoke the recent spool of images—Didier touching me, kissing me. It would be hard to look at him without thinking about those things. I pulled off my sweaty nightgown and tossed it on the floor.

Dalton rolled over and felt me naked next to him. "What's this?" His warm hands pulled me close to his body, tucking me inside him and letting out a long *mmmmm* from half-sleep. I could feel my husband suddenly getting aroused behind me. It was so unlike him to be spontaneous, and completely uncharacteristic to feel sexual impulses at such an early hour. Maybe he was dreaming too.

Dalton kissed the back of my neck and guided himself in between my legs, pushing slowly inside. "Well, someone's ready for me."

I inhaled, letting my breath seep out slowly so that no false words or wrong names would slip out with it. I had always been wishing for Dalton to make love to me this way. But now, all I could think about was Didier. And instead of feeling guilty or wrong, it felt all right. In fact, it helped. Sabine was right. Fantasies were useful little things that harmed no one. Why not just enjoy them and let them portray some other life that could be lived in private purpose, no forum to allow it, no one to comment on it or judge it.

These ripe thoughts were something I could live with, like summers abroad and the Kama Sutra in my dresser drawer. Certainly, everyone had a fantasy life. Even Dalton. But I had never fully let mine in, too consumed with spousal responsibility and ovulation cycles. I closed my eyes, blurring all reality into abstraction, and surrendered to the unprecedented passion of my husband and the consummate desire for another man.

CHAPTER 19

My thoughts about Didier were suddenly as plentiful and requisite as any of my routines. I saw him at the café each morning and imagined a whole world between sips of coffee. A rich subtext of desire. Francine would drift over, frothy and insubstantial, trying to keep her grip. I would act aloof, my nose in the *Times*, my body feeling the heat of wanting and the weight of laissez-faire journalism. Didier's quick pecks hello were enough to sustain me through the days and global crises.

Dalton was simply becoming other. His own habits were beginning to cloy at me. The way he shook his freshly washed hands dry, speckling the counter with droplets of water like a dog shaking off a good dousing. The way he blew on hot food for minutes on end like a child afraid of scalding. The way he checked himself in the mirror, perfecting every last detail before walking out the door. His predictable breakfast banter. His un-veering baby-making techniques. I was slowly suffocating in the magnified humdrum of it. He was inexorably unchanged, and yet totally foreign to me.

Norma continued to fawn over him, as I imagined so many women did who came into his store—women who were impressed by wit and good looks wrapped in twills and gabardines and heeled in fine Italian leather.

"Mr. Dalton, you always look ready for the red carpet." Norma stretched her smile to even broader proportions.

"Too bad all we have here are hardwood floors, eh Norma?" Dalton shook his drippy fingers over the sink, splattering the surrounding granite. Norma glowed brighter in the wake of his clean-ups, her voice rippling like a toddler in a kiddie pool.

The sound of something crashing to the floor accosted my ears before the image of the broken vase did. But there it was in little pieces—the blue and green vase from Marseille that I bought for its crystal reminder of the sea.

"Dammit!" The *dammit* came out in spite of me. I didn't intend on saying it, though I didn't try to filter it out, either.

"Oh my God! I'm so sorry!" Norma scrambled for the dustpan and brush.

"Luci, please! It's no big deal, Norma, honestly. I've been telling Luci that thing was gonna get knocked over one day or another. It was an accident waiting to happen." Dalton placed a hand on her back, consoling, the sheen of his sleeve unable to reflect on her faded cotton shirt.

"Miss Luci, I'll pay you for it." Her voice calmed by the sudden sleeve.

"That's totally unnecessary." He was speaking for me.

"Well, at least let me get you another one. Where can I find it?"

"In the south of France." My eyes stayed on the shards. A silence filled all the empty, broken receptacles in the room.

"Oh, now I feel really terrible. It was special."

"It was just a vase. Tell her, Luci." Dalton's own glassy gaze searing through me.

"Just a vase." Something that once held a memory. Now, just one of many fractured things.

"You see? Think no more of it." The sleeve lifted, taking with it all weight of responsibility. Dalton left in a flurry, as if escaping a possible onslaught of flash photography.

I held up a hand to Norma before she could drip out any more apologies. "It's fine, Norma."

Norma bent over like a child collecting sea glass on the shore while the dustpan filled with specks of Mediterranean. Dalton would tell me I was petty to mourn the loss of material objects. But every day it felt as if I were losing my already insignificant imprint on a house that Dalton had chosen and filled with belongings. I didn't used to care about things. I let him decide, design. I cared about people, ideas. Over time, his tastes, his choices took over.

I was beginning to miss the signs of my former life: books piled on the floor, colored seashells in ice-cube trays, jewelry in soap dishes. Dalton was clearly responsible for shattering something much more intrinsic to my being than a vase.

It should be an unwritten rule that whenever anyone breaks something of yours, you get to go and break something of theirs in return. A kind of splintered exchange. At the very least, I should make Norma break Dalton's silver-plated golf trophy, or crack a hole in his humidor. Then she'd see the bursting seams of Mr. Dalton's tailored shirt. She'd see him as I do: cautious, perfectionist, controlling, his immaculate, shiny hands flapping in the air, never clean enough, never dry enough; never, ever enough.

My heels clicked loudly against the carpetless floors on my way out, the door closing behind me a little too hard. A certain melancholy crept under my skin as I drove away, questioning if there were enough glue or desire in that house to put the better things back together again.

CHAPTER 20

All heads were bowed, hands in prayer position as the word *namaste* issued from the teacher's lips and echoed through the room. Sabine and I bowed to one another with a wink before rolling up our sticky yoga mats and slipping into our sandals.

"You wanna grab something?" Sabine tugged at her stretchy purple pants.

"Café Antoinette?" Another seemingly innocuous visit to our local café was fine by me.

We made our way to the parking lot, dropping off our bags in the back of Sabine's car and feeling the benefit of an hour's worth of deep stretch and flow. Sabine rubbed a smudge off the car door with the back of her thumb and checked herself out in the tinted window.

"Your car is a beauty and so are you." I gazed at both with real admiration.

"Well, at least I can say I had it going on for a little while, right?" Sabine turned away from the high-gloss vehicle.

"A little while? You'll be outshining everyone for a long time to come."

She nodded absently. "It really is a nice car."

"It's the best. One day I hope to drive something a bit more elegant than the family junker."

Sabine looked me straight in the eye. "I'm sure you will. Now let me buy you an overpriced coffee and something to put back those calories we just burned."

Café Antoinette was at full buzz. Saturday loungers, newsprint in hand, cups of hot liquid balanced at their side, taking in international events, local gossip, and lingering sips of French roast. The sprawl spilled out onto the sidewalk.

I envied the successful alternate universe that Francine Clébert had created. There were certain places that made people relish a momentary escape; this was one of them. Its proof was in the calm, settled gestures, the casual slide into rigid chairs, the gentle *click* of spoons stirring in unmeasured heaps of sugar, the closed-eye swallows and foam-covered lips.

"You okay?" It struck me that Sabine wasn't making her usual sidebar comments.

"Yeah. I'm fine. Just tired, I guess."

"Too much Omar last night?" I wanted the details. They made me feel like anything was possible.

"Omar? No, no. We took the night off."

"Is everything all right?"

"Nothing a good cup of java can't cure."

"Ladies. Your order, please." The French worker behind the gilded cash register came to our table, shifting a piece of thin brown hair away from her eyes and tilting her head to keep the rebel strands from falling back.

"Deux grands crèmes, s'il vous plaît." I shot casual glances around the café to see if Francine or Didier were around. I felt relieved not to see the patron in her Saturday glory, and disappointed not to run into her husband. We took a seat near the counter and the resplendent display of cakes came as a welcome distraction.

"Okay, now I know something is wrong: You're not even looking at the pastry, Sabine."

"You know that asshole ex-husband of mine cheated more on me than a crooked stockbroker in a Ponzi scheme."

"I know. Total creep. Is he bothering you again?"

"No, but when I finally ended it with him after thirty years of bearing up and raising children and swallowing shit for the sake of keeping the family together, I thought I'd ended all the betrayals."

"What happened? Did Omar—"

"—No, no. Not Omar."

"Well, then who?"

"My friggin' six-figure body, that's who."

"I don't understand."

"I got some news from the doctor." Sabine nodded and adjusted her top, giving a slight squeeze to her implants, as if attempting to stand taller in the face of her adversary. "The lymph nodes under my right arm this time . . ."

"My God." My instinct was to hold her, but the server with the flop of brown hair was in front of us, holding forth the steaming cups, a light *"voilà"* issuing from her lips as if revealing some greater, silent truth.

"There's nothing to worry about. You're going to fight this thing again, Sabine. You can do it. I'm here for you, whatever you need. Omar's here for you too. And your sons. We'll do anything."

"Yeah. Sure, kiddo. We'll fight it." Sabine winked and I felt like a child being lied to by a parent and given an ice cream to wash down the lie. She picked up her hot coffee and blew in the cup, as if erasing some piece of fate chalked across a blackboard.

"You can beat this."

"I thought I could win the war with fake tits and a shiny new attitude. What a crock of shit." She took a long sip of her coffee, forcing a laugh. Her eyes welled up. "Well, at least I got to take the new model out for a good joyride. All those years of pent-up sexual tension almost killed me before the cancer."

"Sabine, the war isn't over. It's just another battle." I stared straight into her as if my glare alone could anchor her in some faith.

"Luci?" His voice was suddenly in front of us, newspaper folded under his T-shirted arm, hands tucked in his jeans pockets as if concealing something guilty there.

"Didier? You remember Sabine—we were just . . ." I wished he weren't standing there.

"I must be interrupting you. Sorry. I just wanted to say hello." He sensed the mood.

"No, no, dear. It's fine. I was actually just on my way. Sorry, *chica*. I'm pooped. We'll talk later."

"But Sabine—" I jumped up to stop her.

She gave me a look, warning me not to follow. "Stay. Enjoy. Please." She offered her seat to Didier before heading out of the café, her stretchy clothes looking less elastic, her form reflecting less light as she passed by the window.

"Your friend is interesting. Very confident. *Bien dans sa peau, non?*"

"She is." I adjusted myself in the chair, never feeling quite right in my own skin.

"At the photo show, her boyfriend asked me if I would make a portrait of her. Amusing, no? He was seeing all these pictures of suffering children and he asks me to photograph his girlfriend."

"I think you should do it."

"Seriously?" He crossed his arms and stared at me.

"Yes. Seriously."

"But why?"

"Let's just say that Sabine also deserves more time and more respect."

A satisfied grin resumed on his face. "If you say so. I'll talk with the boyfriend before I leave."

"So, when are you taking off?" The reminder of his departure felt cold and numbing compared to the feeling of an imminently greater loss.

"The end of June. One week in Paris, and one week in the south to see my parents."

"The south?" My attention perked. "I'll be in Arles with Jacqui then."

"I'll be very nearby to there. We must see one another!"

A "yes" crept out, unsolicited. I imagined a day with Didier sipping wine under the shaded fruit trees of Provence. The length of a day together would feel enormous. But the rest of my life without Sabine—that was too huge, too unimaginable.

"Excuse me, Didier. I need to go—I forgot tell Sabine something." I rose from the table, the untouched coffees like steamy placeholders of unsaid words.

"Luci, is she all right?"

"She's fine. Why?"

"She has the look."

I froze in my tracks. "What look?"

"A kind of surrender. In the eyes." Didier paused a beat. "She had it just now. Is that why her boyfriend wants a portrait of her?"

My head shook, no more discussion left in me. "I'll see you around."

I averted my gaze as I walked away, lest he should observe something in my eyes as well: a terrible fear, an insatiable longing, and no chance of surviving, either.

CHAPTER 21

Dalton tossed the day's clothes across the bedroom furniture, making it appear like an elegant party had just taken place, all the guests slipping free of their finery and moving the festivities elsewhere. "How was your day?" The shoes abandoned, then the tie.

I wanted to tell him about Sabine. "Just fine."

"Good. Listen, I'll just take a quick shower and then meet you in bed. We're day twelve, right? Did you check your temperature?"

"Day twelve, yes. Temperature good. Ready for takeoff."

"Hon, don't be like that." He stopped mid-button.

"Sabine is sick again."

"What?"

"I saw her today. Doctor says the cancer is back." It came out emotionless, detached, like a loose button from a shirt.

"Shit. Honey, I'm so sorry to hear that. How's she taking it?" Half-naked concern pitched his voice into empathy.

"Like Sabine. Deflecting it, mostly. But I can tell she's scared. She doesn't want to battle it out again."

"I get that. Sometimes I think people shouldn't go for all those huge medical interventions. They can wear you down as much as give you hope. Nature should just take its course. I don't know that I could go through all that. I think I'd choose to live out my last days the best I can, instead of taking all those drugs."

"Seriously? You wouldn't fight?

"I'd probably vote for euthanasia before I'd put my body, my spirit, and my family through all that crap."

"Well, I'd fight back with every last breath. Of course, I apologize in advance for any burden this may cause you."

"Scoff now, but I've seen people go through this, and it's rough. God willing, neither of us will ever have to."

"Chances are, we will."

"Not a really good topic of conversation before sex, is it? Now let me go clean up and we'll switch gears." A towel flopped over his shoulder as he stepped away.

This was the last chance we had to get pregnant before summer vacation—a reprieve of four marvelous weeks without fertility rituals, pills, testers, or thermometers. Each failed attempt at conception was a mini-death. Sex. Death. Birth. How we jumped from one to the other. I felt the menace of all three, always ready to morph to the next.

Sabine was my only true friend in this town. We were two misfits with a thread of complicity and subversion. We could step in and out of Scarsdale as if we belonged, each of us knowing that we were tethered to other places: Her to Long Island and the working-class fishing town where she grew up, me to France and the lash marks it made on my psyche. Very divergent worlds that met up in a posh New York suburb that masked the fishy smell with foreign perfumes and tattooed Romance languages across its storefronts.

What would happen if Sabine weren't here anymore? Who would fill that terrible void of our collusion? I shook the thought from my head like a pair of Dalton's socks flung across the settee.

He emerged from the bathroom, a dewiness clinging to his skin as if intentions were pure. But the grit wouldn't wash from my thoughts.

"Dalton?"

"Yes?" The towel worked its way over his hair, taking out the extra bits of moisture.

"You said you'd prefer to let nature take its course and not use any interventions."

"So?" The loose, wet strands of his mane already getting combed back into submission.

"Then why don't we let nature take its course with us too? Why do you want me to start a harsh drug cycle and artificial fertility treatments? It's a lot for my body. Why can't we just try on our own and if it happens, great, and if not, then it's not meant to be?"

Silence. A look that censored itself. The beginning of a word. "Fine. But if you recall, we've been trying to let nature take its course. It isn't working. If you don't want to have a child with me, Luci, just say so."

"That's not what I'm saying. I'm just tired of all the pressure. We have no love life. It's all about the baby."

"Okay. Let's forget it for now. You and Jacqui will go on vacation, get some downtime, and then we'll try again when you get back.

Let nature take its course. Fine." He slipped into his pajamas as if to prove a point.

"Dalton, we can still try tonight if you like." My words issued with no salve to them.

"Let's just get some sleep. We both need the rest."

As the lights went out, guilt as cold and calculated as our rituals crept into the bed. I had a sudden sense of relief. Because deep down, I wasn't sure if I would fight with every last breath for the life of this marriage or its stubborn, unborn child.

CHAPTER 22

DALTON WAS SOLICITOUS, ready, lips wet, ordering up the first round of drinks. He handed the single malt over to me.

I took a deep sip. Beer was my beverage of choice in the city, far from the fancy vintages decanted at Scarsdale dinner parties. I could breathe with a beer in my hand. Wine made me look like a poseur. "I like this place. It's quite a scene."

"That's funny. You never used to like this place." Dalton smiled and waved to a familiar face down the bar.

A group of youthful, well-heeled women bumped and clustered together at the door, their bursting sensuality cloaked in dress code. They huddled their way in, shedding layers of Burberry over to the bar.

"Hey, aren't you the guy from the shoe store on Fifty-fifth?" A dark-haired woman with an enticing frown eyed Dalton cautiously. Then me.

"Indeed, I am." He reached into his lapel to retrieve a card. Another automatic response, like holding open a door.

"Hey girls, this guy's store has shoes you can't find anywhere else. All high-end imports. Right?" She looked over at me for backup.

I took cover in my beer.

A woman with a thick Long Island accent and black rectangular eyewear piped in. "So, like he's in *shoe business*? Well, you know what they say. . . ."

The band of women broke into clichéd song, trotting out their worst Ethel Merman. Their imitations crumbled into peals of bullish laughter while Dalton conducted the choral with a commanding finger. Soon business cards were being distributed all around, name brands being dropped, Dalton picking up each one.

"Now I see why you come here." I scooped up some bar nuts as Dalton shuffled the cards into a neat stack and tucked them into his pocket.

"Showing up at the neighborhood drinking hole is always good for business. And you know women: They think when a man sells women's shoes, he knows where they're coming from."

"And where are they coming from, dare I ask?" The judgment in my question could not be stifled.

"From a place of wanting attention. Women don't buy expensive shoes to look good for men. They buy them to impress other women." He threw back his drink and waved down the bartender for another round.

"And what about guys?" I was curious what gender theory would come forth next.

"Guys don't operate that way. The ones who care and who can afford it buy expensive things for themselves. Not to impress other men or women. It's pure ego."

"True. Men are huge egotistical bastards. Some even think they have women all figured out." I blinked with exaggerated effect.

He blinked back. "Well, you're not easy to figure out. You're not predictable or cookie-cutter like the women who come into my store or hang at these bars."

"I'll take that as compliment, but I don't think you can pass judgment on every woman. They're not all vapid, you know!"

"No. But they're not erudite, either. The most they carry with them is a leather tote, not a PhD." He pointed to the middle-management crowd in sweater sets around us.

"So, I guess that makes me your intellectual trophy wife." I leaned in with my glass and my haughtiest glare.

He raised his bottle, looking like he wanted to kiss me, but forgot how to in public.

"What are we toasting here?" The brunette was back, lightly swaying her glass in front of us.

"What we always drink to: The death of Wallabees." Dalton, shifting gears.

"The shoe or the animal?"

"I have nothing against the animal. The animal is cute. The shoe is a blight."

"Got it." She raised her wavering glass and tipped her dark head. "My name is Georgia. Nice to meet you."

"Nice to meet you too, Georgia. I'm Luci." I feigned complicity even though I knew this brazen woman was angling in on my husband. It occurred to me that maybe there were other reasons Dalton came to this bar.

"Look. They've got a quartet setting up tonight. You like jazz?" She turned her attention, her body, her cradled glass to Dalton.

"The cornerstone of American music. What's not to like?"

I noticed how easily Georgia was melting into his corner. Dalton tilted his head, letting a spotlight hit the side of his jawline. He knew the power of that jaw.

"I like it too. Bird, Shorter, Miles. All of them." No one was listening to me.

Georgia let the music instantly assault her senses.

I gave an acknowledging nod toward the band, my eyes suddenly catching the smoky stare of the sax player. It was Martin, looking right back at me in his loose Cuban shirt, baggy pants, and Sinatra hat. Dalton noticed my burst of a smile. It was my door opener, my automatic response. He turned to see what was making me so pleased.

"Him? Really? Time to get out of here."

"You can't be serious! There's no harm in hearing him play. He's seen us already. We can't just walk out. That would be so hurtful." I offered a short wave in Martin's direction.

Georgia peeled off her sweater and let herself drift to the sounds of Coltrane. "These guys are really good."

"I'm sure they are. But we really do have to leave. Look forward to seeing you in the shop, Georgia. Luci, let's go." Dalton motioned me toward the door.

I offered a shrug and confused look to Martin and followed my jealous husband into the street. "What's wrong with you?"

"I'll tell you what's wrong with me: Him. He's everywhere. Constantly in my face!"

"Don't exaggerate. You never see Martin."

"But Jacqui does. I don't know why you keep him in our lives."

"He's her biological father, for God's sake!"

"Yes, but I'm her legal father. I'm the one who's there for her every day, who takes care of her every need! Martin's just this bohemian free spirit, playing jazz and living off his family's money. He's a bum. And he doesn't play by the rules. He thinks he can have access to Jacqui whenever it fits his *artistic* schedule. The guy gets under my skin."

"Jacqui knows the role you play in her life. There's no contest there. She just likes seeing Martin. He's like a big playmate for her. They have fun together. That's all." I forced my voice into calmness and reached for his cashmere sleeve. He pulled it away, perhaps sensing my effort.

"This is exactly why I want a child of my own. I don't need some bad memory showing up all over town and laying claim to something that's mine!" He paused under the florescent streetlight, turning him shades of unwelcome green.

"I see." The bar door opened behind me accompanied by a gust of warm, fermented air, emitting a flurry of heat and sound that I wished my own words could release. The saxophone pierced our ears from deep inside, working Dalton's every nerve. "Blue Train" was bopping.

Cautiously, divided, we crossed Forty-second Street and pushed through the large brass doors of Grand Central Terminal, then silently boarded the train back home. Our night, like our intimacy, was abruptly lost, forsaken in a moment of perennial frustration. On the ride back, I looked at the man I had married. Dalton Ames was a successful man, a desirable man. He was a dedicated husband. A legal guardian. And I was his worldly, postdoctoral wife. Yet none of it was quite enough. For either of us.

CHAPTER 23

"What kind of man does that? Is he so jealous of me?" Martin smiled as the last question crossed his thin lips, lips that wouldn't inflate no matter how hard he blew on that horn.

"Martin, keep your voice down. Jacqui's coming."

Jacqui bounded up to the café table, placing a small plate of spongy madeleines down in front of her as if making a bequest of great importance. Martin immediately tried to steal the honors and Jacqui swatted at his hand. "You have to ask first!"

"*S'il te plaît . . .*" Martin batted his eyes like an innocent child and received a token cookie in the open palm of his hand. "*Merci, ma chère!* You are so well raised!" He popped the entire shell-shaped cake in his mouth.

Jacqui laughed and did the same, causing her cheeks to puff.

"Not that well raised. Jacqui, chew please." I wiped the crumbs from the edges of her mouth and shook my head in pretend disapproval.

"So," Martin spoke with buttery crumbs escaping, "this is your little piece of Paris in the suburbs?" He indicated the quaint surroundings of Café Antoinette, which suddenly appeared as unauthentic as a stage backdrop.

"You could call it a token taste of the Left Bank." Irony signaled in my tone.

"More like a hard swallow of right-wing Gaullism!" His eyes darted around the room to the moneyed and branded clientele.

"Mama comes here every day for her coffee because she says Daddy's tastes like sock juice." Jacqui picked at another madeleine with a devilish smile.

I shrugged a confession as Martin and Jacqui laughed. A hand suddenly landed firmly on my chair. I turned to find Didier smiling as if he were in on the joke, the subtle lines in his face holding a hidden parenthesis around his thoughts.

"You seem to be the only ones here truly enjoying yourselves." He stared straight at Martin as he spoke, only extending his hand at the end, as if uncertain of his own punctuation.

"Let me introduce you. This is Martin Deveau. And this is Didier Clébert. His wife, Francine, owns the café."

Martin stood to exchange official, benign greetings in native French.

"So Martin, do you live in Scarsdale too?" Didier's curiosity seemed obviously piqued.

"No, but today is my day with Jacqui and so I came to pick her up."

"Martin is her biological father," I explained in a low French tone, tinting my voice with more shame than intended.

"We're gonna take the train to the city. I love the train." Jacqui, oblivious to my remark, was too rapt by the thought of train travel.

"Me too. I always feel like I'm going somewhere far away. It's like an escape." Didier pulled up a chair, intending to stay.

"That's because you don't have to do it every day. If you did, it would feel far less renegade. Believe me. The subway makes me feel anything but escapist."

"True." Didier turned to look at me. "Speaking of escapes, when are you and Jacqui leaving for the south of France?" He checked his watch as if our departure were imminent.

Jacqui practically bounced on the wooden seat. "Right after school gets out. Then I get to see *Mémère* and *Pépère*. I can't wait!"

"If only my parents were half as indulgent with their children as they are with their grandchildren, I would be a different man." Martin dove in like a gull to steal Jacqui's last madeleine. "You see? I'm too selfish."

Jacqui pretended to be angry, going nose to nose with Martin. Their face-off ended with Martin opening his mouth to reveal the contents gone and Jacqui bursting out laughing.

I looked over at Didier. "We leave on the twenty-fifth. And you?"

"I'll be there only until the thirtieth. Then off to the Sudan. I guess we'll overlap for a short time." Something that looked like satisfaction flashed across his face.

Martin, as if awoken from a spell, noticed the shift. "Are you also going to be in Arles?"

"St. Rémy. Close enough."

"Definitely very close." His eyes darted between Didier's glance and mine. Martin knew me so well he could read a blush whether it were visible or not.

A slender outline in crisp white cuffs appeared tableside. "It's not usual to hear so much French in this place. To whom do we owe the pleasure?" Francine's eyes were fixed on Martin.

Again, he stood, this time leaning in for the requisite peck on the cheek. "Martin Deveau, *papa de Jacqui. Enchanté.*"

Francine responded in kind, introducing herself and her café as one would present an offspring.

"You have a marvelous establishment. Congratulations. And the madeleines are delectable." Martin licked his lips for effect.

"They're my favorite." Jacqui smiled sweetly up at Francine.

"Well then, you must try the *baba au rhum.*"

"Before the conversation gets completely swept away by talk of cookies and cakes, let me give you my number in St. Rémy." Didier quickly scribbled a number on a café napkin and handed it to me. "Now, you can carry on about the pastry." He smiled tightly and a sudden, awkward hush took over the table.

"I'm sorry. I didn't mean to interrupt your conversation. I just wanted to say hello. If you'll excuse me now . . ." Francine backed away like a scolded puppy.

"Very nice to meet you!" Martin called out to her fleeting silhouette.

"I have to go as well. I have something very special to shoot today. I'm sure you'll find it of particular interest when you see it, Luci." He smiled at me and every one of my overly controlled reflexes fought a slight wobble. "Martin, nice meeting you. Luci, Jacqui, *a très bientôt.*" Didier winked sweetly, then walked away, the scent of lemon in his wake.

"We should get going too, Jacqui. We don't want to miss the train. Now, go use the little girl's room." There was an urgent tone in Martin's voice.

"But I don't have to go." Jacqui protested.

"*Vas-y. Allez!*" Martin rarely parented Jacqui or told her what to do. But suddenly he was commanding. Jacqui obediently got up and headed toward the restroom.

As soon as she was out of earshot, he leapt. "So, are you going to tell me what's going on between you and this guy or do I have to guess?"

"Martin, nothing is going on between me and Didier. Nothing. I can assure you."

"Assure me all you want, but you can't deny the look on your face."

"What look?"

"Your heart rate quadrupled when he showed up. You went positively magenta."

"Don't exaggerate. He surprised me. That's all."

"And I think his wife surprised you too. You were quite emotionless when she arrived."

"Martin, you have a very good imagination. They're happily married. I'm happily married. There's no other story."

"They didn't seem so happily anything. He cut her off and made a date with you in St. Rémy! As for your own happiness, I cannot say."

"Then don't. Conversation over."

"It figures that you'd fall for another self-important, entitled type.

Just like Dalton, except French. Seems you've mashed all your attractions into one fancy fellow. Bravo!"

"He's not self-important or entitled or fancy. He's actually a war photographer. And he's heading off to the Sudan to do meaningful work." It even sounded ridiculous in my own ears.

"Or maybe he's off to Africa to avoid his dull marriage to that apparition of a woman. I know his kind. He'll blow into war as he does into a woman's life, like a hot breeze off the Serengeti. Then he'll disappear. On to the next adventure. Believe me. Keep clear of this one."

I wanted to tell him he knew nothing of Didier. He knew nothing of me or my tastes or desires. But before I could answer Jacqui was tableside and Martin was collecting his coat from the chair.

"We'll see you later. Ready, Jacqui?"

"Ready. Bye, Mama!" As my daughter delivered a fast hug, I caught a sweet whiff of mango and orange blossom and longed for the days when my own hair smelled like citrusy, carefree things, instead of the dowdy, stale aroma of restraint.

I lingered over my cup, thinking about what Martin had just said when a specter in white shackles slipped into the seat next to mine.

"Francine—I didn't see you."

"Really? Because I can see you very clearly. And it's more than apparent what kind of men you like. So, I'm telling you now, please stay away from my husband." She leaned into the table with a trembling hand. "Do not call him in France. Do not."

"Francine, Didier is just a friend. I'm married. I have no intention—"

"I don't care whose intention it is. Just keep away. You understand?"

She turned and walked away with a quiver, forcing a smile to the passing customers and leaving me shell-shocked.

Did Didier say something to her? Was she implying that he was somehow drawn to me? Hadn't Martin just noticed the same thing? I studied the napkin with Didier's number on it. It would be up to me if I called him or not. Up to me.

As a sign of good faith, I left the napkin on the table where Francine would see it like a white flag of surrender. But the truth was that soon she would be thousands of miles away and I would have time to decide. Miles of time. One thing was for sure: I would not be coming back to Café Antoinette any time soon. As I slipped into my exile, the warm scent of pastry and the heat of contention ushered me out the door.

My car felt cold and foreign, like it couldn't lead me anywhere good. I dug around the glove compartment, not sure of what I was searching for. But when I had the pen between my fingers, the number I'd committed to memory got urgently scribbled on the palm of my hand. And as my heartbeat quickened, I felt the treacherous potential of the ink on my skin.

CHAPTER 24

We said good-bye to Dalton and the bright greens of June in Scarsdale with a sense of loss for both, knowing that when we returned each would seem somehow less alluring, burned by the workaday week and the oncoming scorch of August. I knew that Dalton resented my summer trips to France with Jacqui. After all, we were going to spend time with Martin's parents. But Nadine and Emmanuel coveted these weeks of indulgence with their granddaughter. Jacqui was pure gold in their eyes, and that alone was worth the trip. Though Martin and I never had a full-fledged relationship, his parents still treated me like a daughter-in-law.

My own parents were too absorbed in their university lives and upcoming publications to be doting on their grandchild. There was a natural assumption that they'd grow closer over time, once Jacqui was old enough to carry on a decent conversation in Middle English or debate the radical ruptures of the Reformation. Mom was stuck in Canterbury, bound by Chaucer and fourteenth-century turmoil. Dad was steeped in European history with its requisite snub and bluster. Jacqui viewed them as oddities, like fanciful antique curios.

Once they gave her a carved glass Victorian pickling jar for her birthday. Jacqui stared at it with total confusion until I suggested she use it to capture lightning bugs. Delight washed over her face as horror overcame theirs. It was clear: Their bond with Jacqui would only ever flower in her postdoctoral years. Same as it had for me.

I sometimes wondered if Nadine and Emmanuel would take on the role of surrogate grandparents if I had a child with Dalton . . . or if we'd still be able to go to France each year . . . if Dalton would let us. Another child could very well compromise these perfect summer escapes and idyllic relations. The constant madness of New York was so much more bearable because of our time in Provence. Without it, we might spend our vacation like so many others, sitting by a buggy lake and mediocre mountain in the Catskills, locked in humidity, covered in Deet and vying for a spot at an overpriced camp. I was beyond grateful not to contend with all that. This was so much more memorable and valuable. And simple.

Nadine and Emmanuel had fixed up the guesthouse as usual, every vase full of wild flowers, every windowsill drying out bunches of fresh lavender, the scent filling the old stone room completely. They always apologized for the size of the cottage, but Jacqui and I longed for this place. It was our tiny paradise. I got to fall asleep each night with the smell of her hair next to me and the warmth of her young, lanky body, changing color each day as it became caramelized by the sun.

CAFÉ ANTOINETTE

We loved everything about the house: its slightly peeling yellow walls, the cracked ceramic pots with bright red geraniums outside the door, the lacey, worn-down white eyelet bedspread, even the bocce-ball court in the garden where we would play *boules* for hours. The game absorbed all of our time to the point of falling asleep in the starchy flowered sheets at night with the echo of balls still clacking in our ears.

We awoke on our first day to the usual ritual: Nadine was tapping lightly at our door. Not waiting for us to open, she entered with her key, looking fresh and glowing like she had just taken a bath in sunflowers.

"*Bonjour, mes filles!* Do you prefer your breakfast in bed or out on the veranda? It's a beautiful day!"

Jacqui jumped from the bed, "Outside with you and *Pépère!* And Yvette too!"

"Yvette is already sitting in the sun waiting for you." Nadine had a lilting, singsong quality to her voice, even when reporting the most benign update on the cat. "And Luci, *chérie*, your coffee is ready."

"*Merci beaucoup*, Nadine." Nadine's coffee was about as far away from Dalton's sock juice as I could get. And it made me all but forget Café Antoinette.

Didier, however, was another story. The sheer proximity to him in Provence made me crave seeing him even more. He was leaving France in a couple of days. I would need to call him immediately in order to see him, and I would have to be careful. Nadine, like Martin, would be able to detect any attraction we had to each other, even if it was harmless. I couldn't bring him by the house. I would have to see him elsewhere. My mind wandered, considering the options and just how far I would take things.

"So, Mama? Are you going?" Jacqui had already slipped on a T-shirt, shorts, and flip-flops and was waiting at the foot of the bed.

"Going where?" I jolted to attention, uncertain if my daughter was reading my thoughts.

"To eat with us." Jacqui looked at me impatiently.

"You go on ahead. I'll be right out." My heart rate steadied.

"But your coffee will get cold." The words skipped out of Jacqui's mouth, repeating a melody more than heeding a warning. It was a refrain she had learned from her grandmother.

I urged a smiled. "Then I'll get ready fast."

Jacqui dashed out the door, forgetting to close it behind her as she often did in her nine-year-old haste, and went sprinting toward Yvette, who sprung up from her soft spot in the sun and shot under the bushes.

I closed the door, rooting around my handbag for my phone. I would call him. Then I would tell everyone I had to go to St. Rémy to see a friend, because it was our only day of overlap. Nadine and Emmanuel would understand. They would relish the time alone with Jacqui.

I splashed my face, threw on some clothes, and headed out to the dappled veranda, the budding day and promise of escape rolling across my mind like colored balls on the earthy lawn.

CHAPTER 25

Jacqui knew her way around the old city, its map imprinted across her childhood summers like a fairy tale told over and over again. "I want to go to Café du Forum for ice cream!" she yelled, darting out in front of me.

I watched her leap from one pumiced stone to the next, never losing her balance on the smooth, slippery rock. My own limbs were decidedly shaky. After all, I was the one about to take a jittery step, as precarious as an awkward girl at her first big dance. Truth was, I had no idea what I was doing. But stopping myself was not an option. I was already on the floor, hearing the beautiful music and spinning.

"You go on ahead and grab our favorite table. I'll be right there."

Jacqui let out a loud hoot, a sound that French girls didn't make, and took off down the street like a veteran explorer launching into high seas. I was always so self-conscious of standing out as an

American. I quickly assimilated to this culture of diverted glances, sullen expressions, judgment suspended on tongues that cradled every word in drawn-out sounds of disenchantment. I was indistinguishable from these people. Yet I was other—belonging as much as any alien plant blown in on a far-flung seedling. I took root and spread. A prairie flower in the big city. Not even my accent could give me away.

My child, however, might. Jacqui was authentic, unconcerned by French protocol. She hooted.

Once my daughter had safely rounded the corner, I stopped to reach for my phone. I dialed haphazardly, waiting for an answer. On the fifth ring, his voice picked up, sounding guarded.

"Allô . . ."

"Didier? Hello, it's me, Luci. Luci Ames."

"Ah! Luci. I didn't recognize the number." His coolness rising to sudden warmth. "I'm so glad you're in the south. What are your plans?"

"We have a hefty schedule of overeating and oversleeping. The usual."

"Perfect! Well, I must see you. Are you available tomorrow? It's my only free time. We could meet for lunch. I know a superb pub in the countryside with the best foie gras. The best. You'll love it."

I could barely register what he was saying, my heartbeat drowning out all language, all reason. I heard myself agree to meeting at noon at the bus station.

"Until tomorrow!"

"À demain . . ." I repeated back.

He could have said anything and I would have echoed. I hung up, relieved and convinced of the amicable intention in his voice, the platonic nature of his suggestion. Lunch. A pub in the countryside. Foie gras. All very innocent. All in the light of day.

I found Jacqui sitting under a shady umbrella with a logo of a popular beverage on it, spiritedly chatting with the familiar waiter. *Our waiter*, as we called him.

"*Madame Luci! La voilà!*" He welcomed me with a clasp of the hand and a tilted smile. "Arles is already too warm, no?" He noticed the slick of my grip, the sweat beading up on my skin. Arles wasn't that warm. But indiscretion has a way of heating things up.

"Monsieur Jean-Marc, how are you?" I willed my internal temperature down to a quiet simmer.

"It's so nice to see my two beauties again! How Jacqui has grown! What are you feeding her in America?"

"French fries." Jacqui giggled, her joy too obvious to quell.

"Of course. Well, the summer never officially begins until I see you both. So, what special treat can I get for you today? Let me guess. Ice cream?"

"Yes!" Jacqui let out another howl as Jean-Marc basked in the glorious, missing social graces of this potato-fed American child, as refreshing to him as a chilled pastis on a hot June day.

It was good to be a regular—to consider anything regular at this moment. It made my pulse steady to know I was on solid ground at our favorite spot on earth with our favorite waiter and about to indulge in a glorious dessert. Probably pistachio. The café only ever served one ice cream flavor per week, and the end of the month was always pistachio. Surely, its sweet satisfaction would help melt away my wobbly self-image. Even self-doubt was becoming regular.

As we waited for our ice cream, it occurred to me that there was nothing terribly adventurous about our time in the south of France. We came for the special comfort of the known. For the tastes and smells and views we were denied the other eleven months of the year. Dalton didn't enjoy these repeated forays. He liked to discover new lands where English was spoken, and not to feel like the odd man out. He liked five-star service and high-design settings and fashionable eateries. He lacked a certain adaptability . . . a certain "get up and go to the Sudan." Dalton was staid and sturdy and predictable. As French vanilla as Scarsdale itself.

"*Voilà! Deux glaces au citron!*" Instead of the putty-green color that I was anticipating, Jean-Marc delivered two pale yellow scoops, one to each of us. Lemon, not pistachio, was suddenly on my spoon, citrus bursting around my tongue and spreading across my palette. I laughed to myself. Even at the end of the month and surrounded by the familiar, perhaps adventure was on the menu after all.

Jacqui picked up a blue crayon from the jelly jar on the table and began to scribble on the paper table cover. I let the rays of early summer kiss my unprotected cheeks, hoping for some crimson, and instinctively reached for the red crayon. Jacqui was filling in a sky with bold, blue streaks tearing across the top of the image. I suddenly felt inclined to muster up some lightning bolts.

"Mama, you're ruining it! It's a sunny day! Now I have to start again." She ripped off the ruined portion of the paper and began to draw on fresh white space.

"Sorry, honey." The ferocious red crayon was surrendered back to the jar, but thunder rolled through my mind. I took strange pleasure in the commotion that Didier was causing.

Jacqui was sketching a garden, a bird, a tree, a cat and a ball, surreptitiously smiling through every stroke. I sat quietly with my tumult of thoughts until she finished.

"That's our cottage and our garden, right? And there's Yvette."

"Yep. Even cats like to play bocce ball."

The factualness of it made me smile. "It's a really nice picture. I think Nadine and Emmanuel would love it. Shall we cut it out and bring it to them? You can sign the back."

"But I made it for you. Except that it's missing one more thing..." Jacqui picked up a peach-colored crayon and drew a small, round figure in the grass.

"A snowman?"

"Of course not, silly! It's a baby."

"A baby? Why did you add that?"

"Because it's what you and Daddy want, right? I hear him talking to you about it."

I was dumbstruck for a moment. "Well, you shouldn't listen in or believe everything you hear."

"So then, Daddy doesn't want a baby?"

I caught my breath. "No, he does . . ."

"And you?" Her stare was so earnest.

"Well, things are great just the way they are, but it could also be wonderful to grow our family too." I took her hand in mine, questioning if anything in my life besides my connection with her was at all great.

"It would have been cool when I was little, but . . ." Jacqui straightened in her chair, adding a small threat of height and age and status.

"I guess we should have asked you what you thought about the idea."

"This is what I think." Jacqui grabbed the red crayon and x-ed out the figure.

I felt the shock of it. Her pain. I had never considered it before. I looked at my daughter and saw her in a whole new light—one that mirrored my own rebellion and also my fear that a new baby would be like rain on a perfectly sunny day.

She filled with tears. "I messed up the picture, Mama."

I pulled her in for a deep, long hug, my eyes glued to the image of our paradise with a big, red X over a newborn child. "You didn't mess up anything, sweetie."

Under my breath, I swallowed the unspoken words: *Daddy did*.

CHAPTER 26

I WAS THE FIRST TO GET UP THAT morning. The sundress I bought in the market the day before dripped over the wicker chair, waiting to transform the hours ahead. But somehow, it seemed too foolish and optimistic—something one of my students would wear, as if by putting it on they were donning a layer of French provincial flesh. It looked more like a disguise. A touristic fashion faux pas, like American women wearing saris in India or Puebla dresses in Mexico. I put it back down and searched for something more geographically appropriate. A serious New York summer statement: a tank top and capri pants. Black. No flowers, no frills. I was, after all, always in possession of a safe, cowardly wardrobe.

The mirror held a distorted vision. Rings of exhaustion circled my sockets. Though I'd closed my eyes all night, sleep couldn't get in. Instead, fantasies came pouring through—so many that they felt absolute. Witty dialogues and flirtatious repartee over sensuous meals with wine and glances blazing. Each scene ended in a kiss that felt so real my heart churned, sweat doused my skin, and slumber became a distant chance whose odds got poorer with each new vision.

Jacqui woke up as I was trying to wrangle my wiry hair into something feminine instead of the warbler's nest reflecting back at me.

"Good morning, sweetheart. Did you have a good rest?"

She rubbed the sleep from her eyes and sat up. "Uh-huh. What time are you leaving today, Mama?"

"Sometime after eleven. Are you looking forward to your day with *Mémère* and *Pépère*?" I was losing patience with my comb.

"It'll be fun. I think they want to expose me to some art or culture or something. But I'm fine with just ice cream."

"I'm sure you'll get your ice cream." I pulled the comb out of my curls with more frustration than I had intended.

"Why don't you just leave it alone, Mama? It's fine the way it is."

Jacqui was right. That was the only legitimate question. Why didn't I leave anything alone? Just let it be. Why didn't I leave Didier Clébert alone? Why didn't I leave my marriage alone? Why did I always mess with things when they were fine just the way they were?

After dressing, Jacqui and I headed out to the veranda for breakfast. Nadine was in the kitchen preparing crepes and the smell of the batter cooking was proof of her devotion. Jacqui followed its scent, yelling "I'll have mine with butter and sugar, please!"

The simple delight of sweet crepes for breakfast is something most Americans didn't know. We settled for boxed cereals and dry toast. Our closest rapport with crepes was pancakes or waffles—its fat North American stepsisters.

CAFÉ ANTOINETTE

I was glad Jacqui was getting exposed to the otherness of France. Not that it was better or worse. Just different. Maybe we all needed to savor the variation of things. Maybe that's what I was doing by spending a day with my intriguing male friend in the charming French countryside. Not that Didier was better than Dalton. Just different. Dalton was golf dates and tee time, wing tips, and eggs on toast. Didier was war stories and foreign adventure, foie gras and crepes. I was ready for otherness, welcoming my day of indulgence with rebellious hair and flowerless clothing.

"Nadine!" I called out to the kitchen. "I'll take mine with chocolate!"

CHAPTER 27

"*Au revoir, Emmanuel. Merci bien!*" I waved my sun hat as I dashed out the car door toward the bus station.

"*Bonne journée, Luci. À tout à l'heure!*" Emmanuel would be waiting for my call later that day to come pick me up. Neither he nor Nadine asked too many questions about whom I was seeing. Perhaps Jacqui would tell them what she knew. Didier was a friend from New York and his wife made the best elephant ears in town. That tidbit alone would set them off on a journey to find the most likely competitor in Arles.

The bus ride was short. Still, I was unable to sit still and found myself in the bathroom checking my reflection in the grimy mirror. Flecks of sweat were beginning to appear on my tank top. I resented them completely. The run to the bus had borne them out. Or was it something else?

I rode out the remainder of the trip, gathering my balance and collecting my thoughts. I had a whole day of escape ahead of me. And it did feel like a getaway, although I didn't know exactly what I was dodging. After all, I was on vacation with my daughter in this beautiful place, well fed and taken care of, no routine to bind me. What more could I want?

The bus came to a heaving halt in St. Rémy. Only a handful of us got off. It was Wednesday and the market was in full swing, bustling with food and wares and foreigners snapping shots of cherries and peppers like they had never seen them before. Colors exploded everywhere as the sellers hawked their goods, offering tastes, deals, promising heaven by the kilo.

I looked around for Didier and saw him making his way toward me through the market swarm, my pulse suddenly driving upward as he got closer. I waved hello, but it wasn't Didier. I diverted my wave to the ground. I felt flushed and foolish and decided to stand under a nearby tree to wait in the shade.

The people going to market happily flowed by me and I wanted to be part of them, to have a purpose and claim what was mine in a straw bag and a pushcart. I suddenly felt adrift, missing the gridlines of my days that kept me on track and focused—the preparation of a meal or a syllabus, the task of nurturing students and loved ones. All of the things that defined me professionally and personally evaporated as I stood under an elm, waiting to be tethered.

Ten minutes passed. Then another five. It seemed too pushy to call, too anxious. I waited. Was he already here looking for me? Suddenly, my phone rang as if answering my query.

"*Allô?*" I tried to shield my frustration.

"Luci! I got you! Hey, how are my two favorite girls?" Dalton's voice took me off guard.

"Dalt? I wasn't expecting to hear from you."

"Why not? I'm your husband, aren't I?" Sarcasm crept into his rhetoric.

"I mean because it's so early there."

"I thought it would be easier to catch you guys now. After work would be too late."

"Of course."

"So . . . how's it going?"

"Great. Fine. Everything is just as we left it." I pictured him beginning his morning rituals, standing in front of the bathroom mirror examining his face, ready to whisk away any shadows that had crept in during the night.

"What are you guys up to today?"

"Today? Not much. I—well, I just arrived in St. Rémy."

"Is Jacqui with you?"

"No. No, she isn't. It's—um, it's market day and I wanted to come and do some shopping. It's so beautiful here. Then I'll grab some lunch and wander around before heading back." I was speaking too quickly, and the half-lie escaped before I could strangle it.

A beat of silence. Distrust? The natural lag of the fragile phone connection? I couldn't tell. "What about Jacqui?"

"She's having some private time with Nadine and Emmanuel. They're thrilled to have her all to themselves for the whole day."

"The whole day? I thought you said you'd be back after lunch. It's probably lunchtime now, am I right?"

"Yeah; no, you're right. I won't be too long. Just want to linger a bit. Nadine will spoil her, I'm sure."

"I'll bet she'll be completely sugar comatose by the time you get back." There was a slight reproach in his tone.

"Yep. It started with crepes for breakfast."

"Ahhh, the French. When will they learn that there is no nutritional value in dough?"

"And when will the health-conscious Americans realize that a month of starch and sugar won't kill you? In fact, it might set you free."

A hearty chuckle came from the other end. *"Vive la révolution!"* Thousands of miles of invisible phone line between us filled with Dalton's sardonic laughter.

A wash of relief came over me, canvassing my prior anxiety. "I'm glad you called, Dalt. And I'm sorry you won't get to try all the fabulous and un-nutritious things I plan on devouring today."

"Me too. It's only been a couple days, but I really miss you guys."

"Well, we miss you too." The statement rang false in my ears. "Call tomorrow at the same time and you'll get to speak with Jacqui too, okay?"

"Will do. Enjoy your day. I love you."

"Me too." I cradled the phone to my sweaty shirt and breathed in a gulp of air tinted with the fermenting scent of fruits left too long in the sun. When I looked up, Didier was heading toward me. Not running, not fretting over his lateness. Just letting the light bounce off his neat, shiny hair and pale muscular skin.

"Luci! *Te voilà!*" He offered a light kiss to each of my damp cheeks, empty of excuses.

"*Salut*, Didier. I thought you might be a no-show."

"Am I late? Sorry. I overslept and then needed to do some things in preparation for my departure."

"I see." I had a torturous night of restlessness while he slept. I raced to the bus to be on time. I stood troubled and telling lies under a tree while he took his time and ran errands. Well, at least I wasn't wearing a silly, flowered dress.

"Have you gone through the market yet? It's wonderful."

"No, I didn't want to wander off in case you were looking for me."

"No one can get lost in St. Rémy. It's too small. I would have found you. In fact, I have one more task to take care of before our lunch. Why don't you explore a bit before it all closes down and then we'll meet?"

Apparently, I came all the way here to play tourist while he packed for his big adventure. The growing noonday heat was dissipating the sweetness of this encounter as fast as pectin from a jar of jelly.

"Fine. Meet you in an hour at that café over there." I walked away as if indifferent. Indifferent to the fact that my limited hours of escape were dwindling, my exercise in self-determination was turning into a battle of self-control, and that I was letting a man I barely knew have such sway over my feelings and fantasies.

I took off through the blurred flux and tints of the market, all my senses acutely aware. Normally, I would have been at my height of pleasure, wandering through a lush landscape in a faraway place marked by ancient Roman and monastic architecture, tracing the lost steps of Van Gogh and witnessing the lunatic colors of his palette. But not at that moment.

I was troubled by my sudden freedom. Uncertain if I had done a terribly wrong thing by coming. I took an uneven breath and my gaze landed on a dark-haired, tawny woman in a provincial dress who was selling necklaces. I went over to see the colorful beads as much as to kill time. The woman gestured as I approached, welcoming me to have a look. Her expression was worn with overdoses of sun and hard life. She could have been sixty or thirty. It was impossible to tell. A true *gitane*.

The gypsies were easy to spot and plentiful down in this part of the world. They were a vital piece of the local culture. Like bullfighters and Impressionists. A large gold cross hung around her neck and took refuge in her generous cleavage, giving the Lord a comfy place to rest.

"*Çela vous plaît?*" She pointed at a handcrafted piece with bright blues and greens, colors that always called my attention.

"*C'est très jolie . . .*" It looked like the sea with its aqua tones and wavy patterns on the beads and made me think of my broken vase.

"You could use some color." She smiled, not intending an insult. She was right. Even a gypsy burial was less morose than my blunt urban style. She looked me up and down, then held out her thermos, offering me some coffee.

I said *yes*. After all, this was my getaway: an invitation to drink Turkish coffee with a gypsy at the market. Wasn't that tantamount to an exotic adventure? Except that it wasn't. It was just coffee. And small talk. She asked the usual questions, made the usual surprised comments on my French, claiming she thought I was native and that Americans never speak good French. I had all my answers down. It was a conversation that I'd had a thousand times. Even if I faked my way through the language, I could have nailed this conversation without a hitch. It had become rote, like so many other things.

I revealed to her that I was on vacation with my daughter, though mentioning nothing of a husband or a delayed secret rendezvous with my neighbor. She complained of the heat and the paltry sales at the market compared to other years. When the U.S. was down, the world was down, she said. I felt the burden of my heritage.

Handing her my coffee cup, I inquired about the price of the necklace. Even false hope was better than none at all. Maybe I would get one for Jacqui as well. She fell silent. Instead, she stared quizzically into the muddy dregs of my empty cup, her deep-set eyes reflecting the color of the grinds. She lifted her gaze to mine as she spoke directly, matter-of-factly.

"Keep your secrets to yourself."

"Excuse me. What secrets?"

"I wouldn't know. Just don't reveal them to anyone. Especially him."

"Who?"

"The one with the big teeth. He is waiting to bite you."

I smiled and flipped my hair in front of my face to protect myself from further scrutiny. "Is that what the coffee says?"

She shrugged. "Seems to be."

I pictured Dalton, Didier, and Martin. Who of the three had the biggest teeth? Dalton had a beaming smile—that of a true salesman. Didier's lips were slender and his teeth average and not very showy. Martin, perhaps, had the biggest teeth. But why would he bite me? It made no sense. Why was I even dignifying such an absurd comment by a strange gypsy woman, or putting any weight in the reading of coffee dregs? I changed the subject.

"And the necklace?"

She was about to answer when suddenly there was a hand on my shoulder. It had a familiar weight to it.

"Hey, I finished quickly and decided to come look for you. I told you no one can get lost in St. Rémy." Didier stood there, wearing his thin grin. "Pretty necklace."

"It's twenty euros." She was trying to get a look at his teeth.

"You like it?" He squinted at me innocently.

"It reminds me of the sea."

He pulled out the twenty euros and handed them to the woman. "*Voilà*. A little piece of the sea and a remembrance of St. Rémy. My gift to you."

"Didier, that's totally unnecessary."

"Do all gifts have to be necessary?" He had look of benevolent superiority.

The gypsy smiled. "More men should be like that with their women."

"Oh, but we're just friends." The words came out of my mouth before I could change their course.

"Either way . . ." As she placed the necklace in a small mesh bag, Didier stopped her.

"No, no. We won't need that." He took the necklace from her and slipped it around my neck. I lifted my hair to clear a path. The beads felt cool to the touch, as did his hands as they lightly brushed over my skin, barely making contact. I must have blushed. The gypsy noticed.

"See? You needed a bit of color." She smirked at me and I noticed a gap tooth in the side of her mouth.

"Perfect!" Didier admired his work.

"*Au revoir, les amis!*" The woman ran a dark tongue over her faulty smile, seeming to put special emphasis on the word *friends* as she bid us farewell. I walked away, thinking only about teeth.

CHAPTER 28

Though most of the world seemed to prefer dining alfresco, I always opted for an indoor setting where I wouldn't have to contend with stray animals, oncoming traffic, or smokers. In Manhattan, garbage could be piled up on the street corners next to a charming café and still the people would sit outside. Trucks and taxis would hurtle by, madly dashing pedestrians would zip along the gum-stained pavements dodging collision. Pigeons, dogs, cats, roaches, and squirrels would alight on the scene, and still diners would be outdoors. I never quite got it. Maybe because my life took place in suburban calm—clean, green settings that didn't vie for public attention. But in St. Rémy, eating alfresco was a local tradition and I happily obliged.

The courtyard where Didier and I ate was small, cobbled, and thankfully shaded. Flourishing, old strands of ivy clambered over the interior walls while grapevines laid claim to the trellised roof, giving a sense of idyllic indoor space punctuated by a sweet hint of fruit. Pots of pansies and impatiens dotted the terrace in glorious summer fuchsias and reds, purples, and yellows. Bees made their way from petal to petal collecting nectar, then moving on to pollinate the next unsuspecting flower. My head was buzzing in the density of this floral enclave. I wasn't sure if it was the thick, external heat or chilled rosé wine that was affecting me most.

"I told you it was the best foie gras ever. Don't you agree?" Didier was in heaven, enjoying every rich bite of liver paste smeared atop a small, hard piece of toast.

"You're right. It's very good. But I think I prefer the tapenade. It's lighter."

"Ugh. You Americans! Always going for something light. Why can't you accept the gravity of things like politics and food? Gravity makes you think, react. Lightness makes you superficial. I can assure you that tomorrow I will be headed to the gravest place I know. It's hell on earth. People there would die for a crumb of this food or a drop of this wine." He held up a glass of water and considered its potential. "This water alone is worth a fortune. We never consider its consequence. We take it completely for granted." Then, raising the glass in a toast, he proclaimed, "To the gravity of living life!"

I took a big, exaggerated bite of my foie gras in complicity, then raised my glass to his.

"You know, I'm glad I met you, Luci. You're different. You understand me. I think those people of Scarsdale, they live in such a bubble. They don't want to see reality."

"Maybe you should give them a little more credit, Didier. Not everyone who lives with opportunity is blind to suffering."

"You're very compassionate. But if you'd see the level of poverty and war that I've witnessed, then you'd think differently. You'd think the entire privileged world was not only blind to suffering, but inured to it. There are enough resources and capital on this planet to fix all of the problems, and still, we sit back and do nothing."

"At least you're doing something. What do you say when you come back, we'll do another exhibit of your work and let Scarsdale be a witness to what you've seen? Maybe this time we can raise funds for children in the Sudan."

"Brilliant idea. If we can reach the people at home, then we can impact a change abroad. For me, it's all about the children. You saw your own daughter's response to the photos. The kids, they get it."

I took a beat, looking him in the eye so as to catch a glimmer of vulnerability, should it flicker there. "I know it's none of my business, but since you relate to children so much, why won't you have any?"

"Who knows? Maybe I will." His spirited discourse stopped short. He quickly downed the rest of his rosé, each gulp like an ellipsis concluding nothing. "There is one last thing I would love to do before leaving for the Sudan. And it will test your true level of compassion."

I tried to read between the lines. "I didn't realize we needed to test that. What do you have in mind?"

"There's a bullfight starting in an hour, and Duchamps is one of my favorite matadors. What do you say?" A naughty smile spread across his handsome face.

I was hoping for deep, lingering conversation laced with innuendo and temptation. He was hoping for conquest of another kind. But after all, he was leaving the next day for months of desperate conflict in hostile environments. How could I deny him a last wish, as superfluous and gruesome as I found it? I threw back the remainder of my wine, steeled myself and said *"Olé!"*

CHAPTER 29

THE OLD ROMAN AMPHITHEater was still serviceable for a pastime that the locals adored with full abandon. Even though Didier grew up in Paris, his summers in Provence gave him a permanent link to this raw, terrible sport. It was in his blood. I could see it from the gleam in his eye as soon as we were handed our tickets. I had been to bullfights before, but never took much pleasure in them, holding my breath, waiting for a young man to be gored or a bull to get speared. Neither outcome enthralled me. Not so with Didier and the hundreds of spectators pushing through the turnstiles in the midday heat, pulses throbbing.

We found seats in a shady part of the arena and watched the warm-up events. Those consisted of a dozen men of all ages in bright white slacks and fitted white T-shirts taunting a series of bulls, one by one, and escaping their charges by jumping onto the barricading wall. There were so many close calls, near encounters, and gravity-defying leaps out of harm's way that, at first, they seemed superhuman. After a while, though, they began to feel strangely normal. Daringly predictable. Soon, my shrieks turned into quiet sucks of air, as if the most lunatic behavior had suddenly become mundane. As if the day might become infinitely more interesting if someone did, in fact, get hurt.

Over a loudspeaker, a caller yelled out the names of each runner, printed in black on the back of his shirt, allotting points for catapults and brushes with the beast. Amounts of money came tumbling out of the caller's mouth with auction speed as each stunt racked up cash for the most audacious encounters. These local men were not only there to flaunt their bravado, but to make a living of it. This was a true exercise in survival. The men I knew back home might look for a second job like handyman or barista, but never matador. Perhaps this was another testament to French gravitas.

The most senior runner spent most of his time waving his arms to taunt the bull, but getting no reaction at all.

"Why do the bulls stay away from the older men? It's like they ignore them completely." I looked to Didier as if he knew it all.

"The old guys have run the bulls for so long, they are no longer a threat. The bulls recognize them. They smell no fear on them, no aggression. So, they don't waste their time."

"But then how do these men make any money if the bulls are discriminating against them?"

"Ha! This has nothing to do with equal opportunity. That is such an American concept. Here in the ring, it's about deciding what you want, how you are going to get it, and staying alive in the process. There is no other choice but to fight for what you want." He placed a hand on my shoulder as if this were something I should consider.

But I saw the older men in a way Didier couldn't. They were still spry, years of experience behind them, but no longer of interest compared to the fleet, elastic younger set. Wasn't this a fate we all faced? Someday, the battle to stay relevant would turn more pathetic than brave, no matter how many great beasts we confronted. I could wear all the flowered sundresses and beaded jewelry that I wanted and still not register a blink in the eye of my intended target.

Didier was glued to the arena, practically jumping the walls himself, cheering the names of his favorite players, yelling instructions at them. For a moment, I was suddenly struck by gratitude that Dalton never took an interest in spectator sports.

"You seem to know so much about this. Have you ever tried it?" I wanted to get his attention. Even for a moment.

"Long ago. It was the best summer of my life. And the worst." He shook his head as if dislodging the memory. "I realized my true passion in life was running with the bulls. I also realized that my father would never let me do it. When he found out what I was up to, he threatened the organization to have them banned for allowing minors to compete. He was a very good lawyer. They didn't doubt him for a second. I was ousted and asked never to come back again."

"That's too bad. But I can't say I blame your father for not wanting you to get hurt."

"It had nothing to do with getting hurt. It had to do with social status. Running in the ring is considered low-class. We are from a respectable family. My father had no issue at all when I left to photograph war from the front lines. Photography was not the trade he would have chosen for me, but at least it was civilized."

"Well, what would he have chosen for you?"

"A high-level, civil-servant position with job security, excellent benefits, eight weeks of annual vacation, and nice, subsidized lunches. A perfect world."

"Definitely not too shabby."

"Ahhh, but there is the tragic matter of the suit. I'm proud to say that I don't even own one." He seemed proud too, sitting there radiant in his fashionable jeans, thin blue tunic, and sandals.

And what of my venerable husband—a man who lived in a suit, who defined the very word, and wore it to perfection? Dalton was a tailor-made man. Was it such a terrible thing to be vested and tied? Wasn't it simply a sign of professionalism and polish? Didier made the concept seem antiquated, as if the suit had passed its prime in the modern world. As if, like the old men in the ring, its death was inevitable.

I sat through the following two hours, defending myself against the encroaching sun, digesting the overdoses of paté in my system and holding down a sick feeling that, at any moment, blood would be spilled on the dusty arena floor. Didier was rapt with attention to the pageantry in the ring. He chatted animatedly with the men and women around us about past battles, the greatest matadors, the best bulls. I followed the discourse with no room to contribute. I was again an outsider who had mastered a language but not a culture. I was witnessing a passion play for a religion to which I did not belong.

My willingness to be there had expired. My time felt crucified minute by hot, dusty minute. And still, Didier remained enchanted, as if beholding the Holy Grail, ready to catch the blood of the Gods at any moment. I sustained the bruising of my ego and stayed by his side. I wondered if Francine would have done the same, or left him to his own devotions.

By the time the toreros had prodded the bull with their capes, the picadors had lanced their fearful thrusts, driving sharp picks into the bull's neck and muscles, and the banderilleros had spurred on the beast's charges with sticks, the acclaimed matador Duchamps had only to finish the job. He dominated the bull, making daring passes around him, this way and that. Neither man nor beast was ready to give up. The bull stood there stomping, humiliated by the picks in his withers and the jeers of the crowd. He was weak and visibly in pain. Every movement cost him more discomfort. The matador wanted to make the show linger, missing an opportunity for a kill just to get the crowd going. Then, coming face-to-face with the depleted animal, he stared him down as the bull dropped his head in surrender.

Duchamps took no time to thrust his sword up from below the chest and into the animal's heart. For a moment, it felt like a mercy killing. The matador's bright, rose-colored stockings, small black slippers, and gold embroidered clothes belied his dark, murderous intentions. He struck a classic victory pose that echoed through the archives of time and place. All that fancy. That magnificent, sun-glinted bravado. All in the name of some strange cruelty that I would never understand.

"Clean kill!" everyone murmured. "Duchamps is always very clean."

The carcass of the poor, defeated animal was carted off by horses, but not before its ears were cut off and handed out as trophies.

Hundreds of flowers were tossed about with much pomp and circumstance as the announcer's voice droned. Duchamps took his bows while flash photos popped like millions of questions in my head. The zealots around me carried the satisfied look of a fresh slaying.

"It's heartbreaking for you, no? All this butchery." Didier placed a hand on my arm for comfort, his pulse still at a high rev. "But you must understand that the people here actually love and understand the bull."

"But if there's love and understanding, then how can you derive so much enjoyment from its death? That's just cruel."

"It's the roles we have accepted. The matador must always be the killer, the picadors his accomplices, the spectators the witnesses, and the bulls are the target."

"Familiarity makes it feels like an even deeper betrayal." Even my thoughts were sounding somberly clad and American.

"Ah, but that's an important lesson, no? Betrayal is usually committed by those most loving and familiar. Otherwise, it's meaningless." He ran his fingers through his loose, dark hair as if sorting through a tangled thought.

I looked at him, my mind drifting toward Dalton, letting Didier's words swim with deadly, unrecognizable purpose. He was right. Betrayal would have no consequence at all unless trust and devotion were truly at stake. And weren't they always? My own treacherous desires were also less than a sword's thrust away.

CHAPTER 30

We silently found our way to a small, dimly-lit place down an ancient, cobbled path, not too far from the amphitheater but secluded enough from the shadows of angry bulls and mad throngs. The sun was still high in the sky and darkness wouldn't really fall till nearly ten o'clock. There was still plenty of time for a drink and time to decompress.

"Luci." Almost desperately, he took my hands in his. His palms were moist, his blood still coursing from all the excitement. "Thank you for coming with me today. Francine would have never gone." A hint of judgment broke free, anchored to something ironic.

"Well, like you said, it's not for everyone." My heart rate quickened at his sudden touch and an unexpected flush surged through me.

Something like empathy flashed in his eyes. "It's not just that, Luci. You have a curiosity toward the world that is similar to mine. Francine is very concerned with her business all the time. Nothing else seems to matter."

I imagined Francine's heavy financial burdens, her investments, her ambitions to succeed and carry on the family tradition. I saw the weight of the world on her frail little shoulders, bearing up to all she had so boldly taken on. I understood that it was not easy to transplant herself in a new country and drag her world-weary husband along, far from his own concerns. Francine had her passions and she was conquering them one puffed pastry at a time. Maybe it was her success that irked Didier, goaded by it like a lance thrust in the back. I noticed he hunched a bit when he spoke of her.

Still, I said nothing to redeem her in his eyes. I only nodded in a kind of unwarranted collusion.

"If I may ask, why doesn't Dalton come to France with you?" He threw the ball in my court, waiting to see if I would criticize Dalton as well, or disparage the life we had together.

I took a deep sip of my pastis and tried to pitch my voice to a more optimistic register. "Dalton has to work. I get summers off, but he can't leave his shop for a whole month."

"No, but he could certainly come for a week or two." Didier's stare seemed to be seeking out some bigger reason. I couldn't tell him how much Dalton disliked coming to France because of Jacqui's paternal bond to this place, because of her attachment to Martin and what he represented, because of Nadine and Emmanuel and the sense of kinship they created in our lives. None of it belonged to Dalton. He was fraught and undone here, and it made him crave having his own family even more. Honestly, I was glad not to have him along. But I could never tell Didier that.

"Well, he's come here quite often, it's just that this trip is kind of my thing with Jacqui, you know? It's special to have the time together, just the two of us."

"I envy you that, Luci. You have it all: a career, a child, a home life. And still, you keep open to adventure."

"It's a work in progress. On any given day, jobs and responsibilities can seem either lifesaving or soul-crushing. We need to keep room for a bit of spontaneity, right?" I took another long draw of truth serum and tried to stop talking.

"That's exactly how I feel!" He drew his face closer to mine, his eyes widening. "The next months will either save me or push me to my limit of sanity. But not going, not taking this chance—that would surely ruin me."

"I know."

"You always understand."

Then suddenly, it happened. His hand was on my cheek, his lips drawing straight up to mine, planting a kiss gently on my mouth, softly at first. He taunted me with a few small pecks before plunging in for something deeper and fuller and hungrier. I held my breath. He dove in, his tongue finding its way. He tasted like anise and dust. His grip grew stronger around me. A small moan escaped me, in spite of my efforts to contain it.

"Let's get out of here." He took me by the hand and pulled me up. I followed, saying nothing, hearing nothing, seeing nothing, objecting to nothing. I just followed. The loudspeaker in my mind went mute. My whole body abided. He rose like a glistening, beautiful, caped man, and I sauntered behind like a poor defenseless creature being taken to slaughter. This was, after all, what I had been dreaming of.

Wasn't it?

The moments that passed between the café and finding our way back to his cottage melted into invisibility. We hurriedly undid our clothes in the dark room, groping at each other in the fading light. I reached for my necklace. He gently restrained my hand. "Keep it on."

We folded onto the bed, letting loose a flood of desire that had been capped for too long. His body felt lean and strong. His touch was commanding and yet soft. He felt his way across my skin, and I let him do as he pleased. His lips grazed my breasts and belly and I watched him as if witnessing a movie. I pushed away all thoughts of Dalton, all calculations, ovulation cycles and monthly objectives. I melted into this captivating man with no other purpose than making passionate love. That alone felt like freedom, and my body responded like a lifelong detainee whose chains were cut, whose doors were flung opened. I ran wild.

When it was over, our bodies lay doused in sweat, chests heaving, all pleasure spent.

"My God, I have wanted to do that for a long time, Luci." He tenderly kissed the nape of my back.

"Me too." The words slipped out on an exhale, like a confession.

There was no "what now?" or "what have we done?" There was no tongue-tied review of what had just happened. There was just silence and sweet breath and a steadied, singular heartbeat.

His hand slipped into mine. "What time do you have to be back?"

My head popped up. "What time is it? The last bus is at nine-thirty."

"It's almost nine now."

"Then I guess I should wash up." I lifted myself from the sheets, wishing that he would stop me, and that time would languish for a while. Instead, a chill hit my skin like a slap in the face as I walked naked toward the bathroom. The impromptu escape had ended. My otherness was all but gone. I was back to maintaining order and semblance and appearance. I was checking emotions, inspecting body, fixing hair. This matted mess of mine would surely give me away. I did my best to clear away the signs of deviation.

Part of me didn't want to wash off the day, its heat and dust and pleasures. I wondered if his scent were on me, or if his kisses had left marks on my neck or skin. I wanted to keep the exposures of a passionate evening with me. I moistened the small hand towel in spite of myself, trying not to catch my own treacherous reflection in the mirror, afraid that I'd only see flawed judgment. I was feeling anything but flawed.

Didier was dressed when I entered the room and the too-bright light was on. I felt a sudden shame in my nakedness. For the first time, I could see the cottage and it was almost as bare as I was. A small wooden chair painted in robin's-egg blue straddled the corner. A hand-carved walnut dresser with an oxidized mirror stood against the wall. The bed was the only other piece of furniture, and its small size discomfited me somehow more than my state of undress.

Didier pulled a suitcase out from under the bed, his energy already in another gear. "I still have packing to do, and so much to prepare for the trip. Otherwise, I would drive you back."

"The bus will be fine. I know you have a lot to do. I'm just glad we got to spend today together. It was wonderful. And unexpected." I leaned in to touch his cheek.

He straightened. "Luci, I want you to know that it will be very hard for me to be in contact from the Sudan."

"Oh. I know that, Didier. Don't worry." I slipped into my wrinkled clothes, trying to make everything as smooth as possible. "I'll see you when you get back home."

"Yes, of course." He offered my hand a squeeze. Then turned toward the door, opening it for me. "Shall we, then?"

The bus ride was an endless stream of thoughts about his touch, his body pressing into mine, his arousal. There was an odd absence of any guilt. Perhaps because I had played the scene out so many times before in my head. Perhaps because we were two consenting adults. We were friends. Neighbors. Or maybe because we both knew this was our only chance to be together, far from the scrutiny of others. This was our escape from Scarsdale. I looked out the window into the humid night of Provence and felt complete relief.

Nadine was idling in the old Peugeot when my bus pulled into the station. I quickly jumped in the passenger seat, trying not to call attention to my disheveled countenance. "Sorry to be back so late, Nadine. Thank you for picking me up."

She eyed me curiously. "Jacqui is fast asleep. We suffered a lot from the heat today. And you? Did you manage to have a nice time with your friend?"

"Yes, a very nice time. And a very hot time too." I tamed a piece of my frizzy hair back and smiled.

"Good. You can take a nice shower when we get home." She

stepped on the gas and the car lurched forward into the night. "Is that new?"

"What?"

"That. You weren't wearing it this morning." Nadine pointed at my beaded necklace.

"Oh, that. Yes, I got it at the market today."

"Not your usual style. The young girls wear such things."

"I know. But I thought I'd try something different today." I wondered what else she noticed. If she could see the lying, happy, satisfied me, adrift in something beginning to feel like love.

"It suits you."

"Thank you, Nadine." My benign words slipped through the thick air, veiled through tones of familiarity and betrayal.

CHAPTER 31

Boiling, sun-soaked days passed, constantly looking for the shady, the temperate. Long nights of sweltering in bed next to Jacqui. Hanging a sheet in the open doorway and dousing it with buckets of water, hoping that a small breeze would be ushered in. The mosquitoes were having a field day and Jacqui and I both ached for the bug sprays and air-conditioning of home. A heat wave like no other, they said. So fierce that it zapped willingness to do anything other than find a speck of relief at the beach.

It was as if my one night of passion set the world on fire. Didier would not escape my thoughts, barely leaving me room for the attention I usually lavished on my daughter. I felt distant, distracted. I blamed the heat. After all, it was making us all spin off course.

But Jacqui could tell there was something else. She felt my restless sleep. She noticed my easily broken attention, my loss of appetite. I tried to assure her with long hugs, needing the caress as much as she did. Still, she knew. Her drawings turned darker, more abstract. She imagined insects with giant eyes and twisted claws—complicated, tentacled creatures floating in a void. There were no more smiling, sunny skies in her renderings. Nadine also noticed the change and asked her about it.

"It can't be sunny all the time. Sometimes living in the dark is better." Jacqui's response was matter-of-fact.

I wondered if it were true.

Then there was Dalton. He was calling too often. The house was so empty, he said. Norma had nothing to clean. All of our friends and neighbors were on vacation or visiting their kids at summer camp. No one was in town. He wanted us back. I found myself annoyed at having to fill so much of his airtime with pleasantries. It somehow soured my days to recount my activities. Like he was keeping tabs.

Until one day, suddenly, the phone didn't ring at all. Not once. It was strangely relieving. But by midnight, I was concerned. It was Saturday. Normally, he would have called first thing in the morning. But it was already early evening back in Scarsdale.

I dialed. The phone rang several times, in no rush to be answered. He picked up in the middle of a laugh.

"Dalt? Is everything okay?" I could hear music in the background, which muted as he began to speak.

"Hey, babe. Everything's great. What's up?" His distracted tone took me off guard.

"Am I interrupting something? Sounds like you have friends over." I imagined Larry Klinger or Jay Miller lounging in the den, drinking beer.

"No, you're not interrupting. I'm glad you called. Now I get to say good night to Jacqui."

"Jacqui went to bed a long time ago, Dalt. It's midnight. Who's there with you?"

"Here? Well, it's just me and Norma." A familiar voice echoed through the background.

"Norma's there? Mondays are her days to clean. Why is she there on a Saturday evening?" I tried to restrain the accusation in my tone.

There was silence on the other end. I could sense Dalton moving to another room. His voice returned, more hushed. "Listen, I asked her to come on Saturdays to iron my shirts. She does a beautiful job. So much better than the dry cleaner."

"And why did you have to tell me that in private?"

"Because I don't want her to feel like she's a domestic."

"But she is a domestic!"

"Luci, don't get worked up over nothing. She's been keeping the house so nice for you, and it's good for me to have some company here. Plus, it's helpful to have a home-cooked meal once in a while. I'm sick of takeout."

"So, now she's cooking for you too?"

"What's the big deal?"

I imagined Norma preparing a beautiful meal for Dalton, then trying on my glass slipper and dancing salsa with him through our living room. I wondered what tricks she had in her back pocket, ready to be pulled out whenever the lady of the house was away. And yet, after what I did with Didier, was I allowed to be jealous? Didier was cultured and worldly, smart and good-looking. But somehow Norma felt like a bigger threat. She was young and pretty and willing to please.

"Dalton, I just don't feel comfortable with you spending Saturday night having an intimate dinner with our cleaning lady who—frankly—has always had her eyes on you!" The words came out emphatically, hypocritically.

Again, there was silence. "You're overreacting. And you've just blown a very simple transaction completely out of proportion. You want me to tell her to leave? Fine. I'll tell her. But she'll know that it's because of you."

"Dalton, just step back and see it the way anyone would. It's inappropriate to be having dinner for two with the help."

A puff of angry, disapproving sound emitted from the other end. "I guess being in France has brought out the classist in you, Luci. I cannot believe you just said that."

He was right. It sounded awful and I knew it. But I couldn't help myself.

"It's not a question of being classist. I'm drawing a line where it needs to be drawn. Should I invite the gardener out for drinks?"

"Do whatever you damn please. This whole conversation is insulting and ridiculous. Good night." And then a *click*. Dalton hung up. Just like that.

I was left with a sick feeling. I knew I should call back and apologize, but I didn't. It was best to leave it alone. But the question of Norma continued to gnaw at me. I would definitely have to fire her when I got home. It would be too awkward to keep her on. Dalton would be very upset with me, but she would have to go. In the same way Francine Clébert had expelled me from Café Antoinette, I would have to protect myself, my family.

CAFÉ ANTOINETTE

I slipped quietly on top of the bed next to Jacqui and tried to close my eyes in the thickening heat of night. But all I could see were images of Dalton and Norma in our climate-controlled home, laughing, drinking, eating, making love. I tried to think of Didier, to invoke him like a God, like a prayer in my time of need. But no image would come. Just my husband and my housekeeper.

Dalton always liked to do it when we were squeaky clean and Norma was the goddess of spotlessness. I imagined her sanitizing every surface in the house before they desecrated it together. Countertops, tables, rugs, bathtubs. The tighter I closed my eyes, the more visceral the scenes became.

The details of my own betrayal were fading fast, like a love letter whose words went missing, afloat in a bottle somewhere far off the coast of dusty, dirty Africa.

CHAPTER 32

A COOLNESS SLIPPED INTO OUR conversations from that point on. Dalton didn't mention Norma again and neither did I. Instead, I would say a few words about my day with Jacqui, then quickly put her on the phone with him. It was a formula that worked for everyone. From time to time, I asked about the mail. If there were any cards, letters, anything of importance that I should know about. He would have mentioned an airmail stamp. But there was nothing. Not a single word from Didier.

I knew it would be difficult to be in contact from the Sudan. But was it impossible? What if something happened to him overseas? How would I ever find out? He must have known I was concerned for his well-being. After all, we spent his last night wrapped up in each other's arms and tangled bodies. That had to mean something.

Or maybe for him, our moment of intrigue was nothing more than an impulsive connection between two friends. I reviewed everything he said to me, every word, reminding myself that sometimes men say things without realizing how women hear them, or the value placed on them. I gave too much weight to Didier's words—words like "you understand me." And yet, I also needed to protect myself from getting hurt, and to guard what I already had. I wasn't ready to lose Dalton. He could not find out what had happened.

Neither could our friends and neighbors back home. It would poison the well and everyone would sympathize with Francine. I would be ostracized. I was already considered insurgent for having a full-time career. Stealing the French pastry-maker's husband would oust me completely and probably put me right back in Manhattan with all the other sinners and deviants. But mostly, I needed to retire any thoughts of Didier for Jacqui's sake. I could never explain to her the power of lust or the impetuous decisions made to satisfy ego, body, desire. I would have to erase Didier Clébert from memory: his touch, his scent, his weighty words. All of it.

At least, that was what I kept telling myself. Until his message arrived.

My phone vibrated on the table, and I went to pick it up, waiting for Dalton. Instead, a text message appeared from Didier. Those few lines, benign as they were, set my heart ablaze all over again. He was having an incredible experience. The people and the place were changing his life, his perspective. He was thinking of me. *Thinking of me.* There it was.

I waited before composing a response. After all, I had spent significant time expelling his spirit; I didn't want to invite him back in so hastily. I finally wrote something distant and careful that ended on a casual, but kind, note. After I sent it, I questioned if a dose of enthusiasm and wit would have served me better, or at least tempted him to write me again. Maybe he was also waiting for a sign.

But my response tempted nothing. Again, he fell into dead silence and I became the wanton teenager checking the phone all day. He was back in my blood. A scarcity of phrases, noncommitted lines pecked out on a phone, and he was under my skin, obscuring my view, controlling my synapses all over again.

The heat finally broke and with it came almost mistral winds, puffed up by cool air off the sea. The shift felt as sudden as my mood. I spent every moment outdoors, swept up by the inconsistent breezes. The gusts carried heavy loads of airborne particles, pollen, and sand. But I sucked up oxygen in big gulps, hoping to sober my mind, calm my heart, breathe.

I threw myself into an ambitious gardening project with Nadine, who was grateful for the company, as Emmanuel was too busy playing *boules* all day with Jacqui. I spent hours on my knees, pruning away at plants, deadheading flowers, preparing for new growth, new life. The torpid heat of the summer had all but burned everything out. It suddenly felt like there was a chance of survival.

I potted chipped porcelain containers with small bursts of roses and hydrangea. I severed large, overgrown ferns and moved the cuttings to different shady areas of the garden bed, filling in the gaps, embedding my fingernails with earth as if I'd just crawled out from the grave. I buried the past, my affair with Didier, and looked for forgiveness. Because this was what gardening was really about: Forgiving. It was a true exercise in clemency—figuring out what should stay, what should go, if something should live or die, be cut back, or left to thrive.

Toiling in the ground brought me an unanticipated clarity, even empathy. I was glad for it. There was no wavering about what to do. Even the wrong things were right and necessary. They were lessons learned. Places to begin again. I never wanted to leave that garden or Nadine's company or the sound of Jacqui blissfully clacking balls on the grass court with her grandfather. I wanted a death-row pardon, and to stay.

Hands and knees doused in dirt, I paused to take in the bucolic view, lit in the yellow of magic hour as if Van Gogh himself had painted it. I could see how landscape and love could bring someone to fits of madness. This place made me so happy and so terribly torn at the same time. It made me yearn for something more, something infatuated and worth mourning.

The thought of returning home was officially souring my stomach, provoking a sudden daily bout of indigestion. Nadine was concerned I had picked up a parasite from eating food from street vendors whose provisions had endured the extreme temperatures. I had a weakness for crepes and crusty sandwiches. I assured her it was just the usual onset of nerves that came with the approaching academic year, the pressures of my workload.

What I failed to mention was how much Dalton influenced that load with his unstoppable quest for offspring. According to our deal, I would be starting with more aggressive fertility treatments when I got back. The thought alone made me seize up. Nadine brought me a cup of tea to settle my stomach.

CAFÉ ANTOINETTE

I went inside, washed the lusty earth from my skin, and sent Didier a text. It was a restrained note saying that I was leaving Arles, heading home, and looked forward to hearing from him soon. A simple return message of *bon voyage* came back within the hour. Nothing more. No promise of contact or willfulness or longing. Just *bon voyage*, like an empty vessel being dispatched to sea.

I glared out the window at the setting sun. Men, love, forgiveness—it was enough to make me lunatic. As a flurry of conflicting thoughts assaulted me, I wondered: When someone cuts off an ear, do they continue to hear punishing internal dialogues, or just sink deeper into the pain of silence?

CHAPTER 33

I SAW HIM STANDING AT THE gate, looking neat and sharp, a pinched expression on his face like something smelled rotten. Jacqui caught eyes with him instantly and ran the remaining thirty yards straight into his arms, nearly bowling him over. I kept my pace until we were in front of each other, offering a light kiss on the lips, a loose, isolated hug, which could be blamed on either the cumbersome baggage I was holding or the tight smile he gripped. Either way, my heart sank.

This was our joyful reunion, filled with untapped resentment, tacit words better kept locked in suitcases or repressed in calculated phone conversations. My actions that summer had made an irreparable tear mark in my relationship with Dalton, whether it was my true intention or not. In seeking some kind of reprieve from his indifferent maneuvers and staid objectives, in taking a departure from the straight and narrow line that I'd been walking in my marriage,

I'd created a radical rupture. The only question was: Did I want to mend it?

"Here, let me carry those for you." Dalton took the bags from my arms, but not the burden of what they carried. "How was your flight?"

"Guess what?" Jacqui was buoyant with excitement. "Mama threw up in the plane!"

Dalton looked at me as if to confirm. I nodded in collusion. "I caught a stomach bug. Some kind of parasite. It should clear up within a month."

"Can't you take anything for it?"

"I'll see a doctor."

"So, I guess that means we wait another month . . ." A frustrated sigh escaped his already disappointed lips.

"Wait a month for what? Are we going somewhere?" Jacqui looked at us with confused curiosity.

"No, we're not going anywhere. Daddy means wait a month before we can get back to feeling healthy and strong."

"Well, I feel healthy and strong, so Daddy and I can go out and play while you hang out in the bathroom." Jacqui practically skipped as she spoke.

A defeated look escaped him. "I guess so, sweetie."

More than ever, I was feeling like the petri dish in which Dalton's dream-child could incubate. I had hoped that he wanted to make love to me out of desire, out of relief for having been one month apart. But agenda drove him more than love or libido, and when we crawled between the cool sheets that first night, almost like strangers, he made no move whatsoever.

I stared at the ceiling, incapable of initiating anything, and feeling as if he might be able to see through false affection should I attempt. The long-desired air-conditioning that I'd dreamed of all summer was now a frigid microclimate surrounding us in polar extremes. I missed sweating between the sheets with Jacqui by my side and thoughts of Didier between my legs.

Dalton rolled over to offer a compensatory hug. My body tensed up.

"What's wrong?" He sat up.

"It's just so damn cold in here. It's like a goddamn icebox!" I jumped out of the bed and frantically rummaged around for a sweatshirt and socks. The additional armor proved useless as, in my haste, I jammed my foot up against the wooden bedpost and bellowed a string of obscenities.

"Are you okay? Can I get you anything" Dalton leaned over to inspect the damage, undoubtedly looking for a bloody trail.

"It just fucking hurts." There was blame in my tone and he caught it. "Why is it so freezing in here anyway?"

"I'll go turn the air down." He looked at me as if I were crazy, exaggerated, absurd. Like an hysterical woman jealous of her housekeeper, or willing to give up her perfect suburban life for a fly-by-night Frenchman.

He lowered the air and within moments the room began to swelter. Dalton grabbed his pillow and went to sleep on the couch downstairs where it was cooler. I stripped down to nothing and simmered in the familiar heat and solitude.

CHAPTER 34

THE SHARP SMELL OF MEDICAtion reached me before the sight of her did. But there she was, propped up in a special bed in the living room, her hair done, makeup impeccable. Same old Sabine. Just worn down.

"Well, if you ain't a sight for sore eyes. I'd say someone needs a salon day. And it isn't me." She looked me up and down from her elevated position in the room.

I walked over to offer a bent embrace, wishing I could slip under the covers and share my secrets instead. "I missed you, girlfriend. Here. A little something from the south of France." I handed her a provincial quilted bag full of lavender oils and olive soaps and face creams.

"Perfect timing. I just ran out of the stuff you brought me last trip."

"Well, now you have another year's supply."

A look of irony passed over her face. She stared down at her double-crossing body. "If I only had a year left in me."

"You have lots of years left in you, Sabine. You look great. How do you feel?"

"Not so great. Radiation sucks the lifeblood right out of you. God knows why they call it therapy."

"I'm glad you're following the doctors' orders. I was afraid you'd tell them all to go to hell."

"I did! This isn't because of any doctor. It's because of Omar. He's making me do this. If he only knew what he was putting me through, he'd lay off. But he thinks the treatments will save me. I do it for him. It gives him hope. Can you believe that? My endless nausea and fatigue give him hope."

"But the treatment might actually be doing some good."

"It won't change much of anything. It's just a question of time. But Omar believes in miracles."

"Don't you?"

"I believe in the miracles of cosmetic surgery and fine German engineering." She ran her fingers through her thinning, well-coiffed hair and licked her shiny lips, smiling like a covert operative. "I'm sick of always talking about this nonsense. Tell me all about your trip. How was it?"

"Well, Jacqui and I survived stifling heat and mad windstorms, but other than that, it was terrific. Except this time I got some sort of parasite from something I ate. Must be sympathy pains." I patted her shoulder.

"Oh, that sounds like a barrel of monkeys. Oven temperatures and wonky French food. *Vive la France*. Gimme radiation any day." She laughed and coughed up some phlegm.

"I guess so. But it was so good to escape the usual stuff and get away."

"Back to the grind now, huh? I get it. Well, you know what they say: The best way to break up a routine is do something differently." She winked and raised her water glass.

"I know. Turn left where I usually go right. Shake things up." I shimmied in mock enthusiasm.

"Dalton doing okay?" She stared down a bubble in her water.

"He's upset that we have to wait again before trying, because of this stomach thing I have."

"And what about Mr. Fantasy? He still taking up real estate in your head?"

I sat down on the edge of the bed and leaned in. "I saw him there. We got together the day before he left for the Sudan."

"So, when you say *got together*, do you mean it in the platonic way or the French way?"

I paused, needing desperately to confess. "The French way."

Sabine popped up from her cushion as if propelled by some involuntary motion.

"Well, I'll be damned! Didn't think you had it in you, Luci Ames. Talk about shaking up your routine! That's one heck of a left turn." She couldn't refrain from laughing.

"Don't make me feel worse." My face collapsed into my hands. "What am I going to do?"

"Well, do you care about Frenchy or was it just a flash in the pan?"

"Both, I think."

"Have you been in touch since that night?"

"Barely. Scanty text messages. That's it. I'll have to wait till he gets back in a couple months to see what's up. In the meantime, I've been unsuccessfully trying to delete him from my thoughts."

"Oh, honey, you've got it bad. One night of uninhibited sex can do that to a person."

"Tell me about it." I held my stomach as a sick feeling rose to the surface.

Sabine inspected me slowly. "Nausea?"

"It's just this stomach thing."

"Luci, honey. I hate to say it, but did you ever think that maybe it's not a bug you caught in France? When is the last time you had your period?"

I froze, calculating, the nausea mounting, my fears along with it. "I'm a little over a week late, but sometimes that happens when I travel or when I'm stressed."

"Or when you're pregnant." She looked at me with pity, as if I were a foolish schoolgirl who didn't know a thing about her own body. "Honey, it's a possibility. That's all I'm saying."

"Jesus, Sabine. What the hell will I do if that's the case? I can't—"

"First things first. Don't panic. Do the test. Then you'll know for sure." She was suddenly comforting me, her hand on my shoulder, her voice consoling, her gaze glued to mine.

I stared at her and suddenly knew if I had a choice, I'd take radiation.

CHAPTER 35

I DROVE TO THE LARGE, IMPERsonal pharmacy one town over, instead of my small local drugstore where they knew me by name and might ponder my purchase. There were dozens of brands of pregnancy tests all proclaiming the same thing: 99 percent accuracy. I wished I could do anything in my life with that kind of certainty.

I was blocked in a kind of shopping quandary, not wishing to ask for advice from the pharmacist or call greater attention to my dilemma. I stared for an endless moment at all the boxes, inspecting, trying to intuit which would be the best tester, and the one to give me a definitive negative result. I landed on a pretty blue logo with two testers inside and headed to the checkout, scooping up some gum and crackers on the way, as if the pregnancy kit were just an afterthought. Showing no sign of panic, I asked the cashier most casually if I needed a code for the restroom.

Back behind giant stacks of dried goods and cleaning products was the employee bathroom. I punched the code and slipped inside, hastily reading the simplistic instructions on the tester box over and over, trying to make them more complicated least I do something wrong. But hadn't I already done something wrong?

I held the wand between my legs, squatted and aimed at the stick, my urine hitting the target area like a bull's-eye. I laid the wand flat for a minute and waited. Then waited some more. Nothing appeared in the window. Not even a control line. After all that, I had bought a dud, which made me question the statistics of that particular inaccuracy as well as my own rotten luck.

I left the musty pharmacy bathroom with a heightened feeling of impending bad news. The only thing left to do was drink more liquid and do the test all over again. Going home was not an option. I got in my car with the second tester in my pocketbook and headed to Scarsdale in search of a beverage.

As I passed the entrance to the parkway, I noticed a familiar car at the stop before the ramp. Francine Clébert, a taut look on her face, glared out at the road. I wondered if she were thinking about Didier, or business at the café, or if it crossed her mind whether her husband had slept with the person staring at her from the car opposite. Either way, she was clearly heading into the city and the coast was clear for me to go to Café Antoinette, have a drink and do my test. Somehow, finding out the answer there seemed appropriate.

The café remained a place out of time, suburbanites escaping the summer heat and catching a moment of pretend before returning to the tasks of pickup, drive, work, home. Men and women plucked newspapers from wooden scrolls and peered over international headlines in English or French, surrendering to the inky words and foreign interests. Cell phones were discreetly tucked into pockets or purses, not wishing to break the appearance of a time before technology was portable and ubiquitous. I missed this place, feeling a bit like a trespasser as I walked up to order.

"I'll have a *café au lait*, please. No, wait . . ." The choice of caffeine suddenly felt risky. "Make that a mint tea."

I took a seat with my cup, letting the tea and my thoughts steep. What if I were pregnant? What if Didier was able to do in one night what Dalton was unable to accomplish in four years of marking days and temperatures and ovulation cycles? One night of complete release, no agenda, just a connection between two people. A few hours when heart and mind were linked and I could surrender to the moment, instead of going through amorous motions with counterfeit desires. I wondered what other damages and glories I could perpetuate in this lifetime if heart and mind were always kept in sync.

With the teapot empty and my bladder full, I slowly rose. The bathroom was occupied and stayed that way for several long minutes. Thoughts of what this woman could possibly be doing for so long crossed my mind. But I had no right to judge. I was the cheater, the trespasser, the occupier. I was the one peeing on a stick to find out if two blue traces would change my fate. A teenaged girl finally opened the restroom door, offering an apologetic smile.

I thought about my own teen years, blithe and distant. At least they seemed that way now. Jacqui would be getting her period soon enough, creating that ongoing worry and sensitivity that accompany women through their sexual years. Maybe lots of females hid out in local cafés and took pregnancy tests. Maybe the Dumpsters in the back were full of wands, strewn in garbage piles like unwanted birth announcements.

I did the test. Then waited. There was a knock on the door but I ignored it. They'd have to wait too. Instantly, two streaks, vibrant and strong, appeared. No dud this time. A positive was clearly indicated. At least, 99 percent positive. One percent of me held out for misinformation. For rewind. To relive that night in St. Rémy and change the outcome.

I wrapped the tester in sheets of paper towel and with trembling hands, buried it deep inside the trash. This would not be a happy souvenir to bring home like some long-awaited news. The anxious person with a full bladder jangled the door handle, then knocked more briskly. She was probably thinking, "What could this woman possibly be doing in there?" Little did she know that I couldn't move, couldn't breathe, paralyzed with the fear that as soon as I left that room, my entire horizon would shift. My perfectly routine life, chased away.

"Is there a problem in there?" A voice, laced with sarcasm or sympathy—I couldn't tell which—came from the other side of the door.

I held my stomach and stared at the sink. "Yes. I'm afraid there's a problem. A big problem."

CHAPTER 36

"I don't know what to do, Sabine." I cupped my hand around the phone, though no one could possibly hear me in my car as I sat in the outdoor lot, cowering, exposed.

"I had a feeling. Sorry, kiddo." Her breath grew heavier over the line.

"What a mess. This is just so stupid. I'm a married woman, for God's sake!"

"So then, let me ask you: What are your options?" She was calm. Pregnancy did not sound like a death sentence to her.

"I guess I can get an abortion right away. No one will know. Dalton will think I'm sick from the bug I supposedly caught, so he won't suspect. Or I can have sex with him every night this week and pretend that the child is his."

"Could you really do that to him?"

"It's horrible, I know. But it would give him what he's always wanted."

"I don't think he wants some other man's kid."

"Shit, Sabine. What do I do? I can't tell Dalton the truth."

"You forgot one option." There was a slight scolding in her voice. "Tell Didier what happened and see what he wants to do about it."

"I couldn't possibly inflict that much chaos on everyone. I've done enough. I don't even know if the news would make him happy or send him running. Not an option."

"So, you're never even going to tell the guy?"

"Never."

"Well, then the only answer is to do whatever's in your heart. These are big, irreversible choices. You don't want to live with any regrets. And just know that whatever you choose, I'll support you."

"I know that. No one else can ever know, Sabine. No one."

"Trust me. Your secret will go to the grave with me. Which might be sooner than later. So please, decide quickly."

Always humor in the face of tragedy. That was Sabine's way. We laughed in spite of it all—nervous, guilty, furtive laughter between one dying friend and another carrying a burgeoning new life.

A light tap on the window made my heart jump. "Call you later."

Shari Miller, in expensive workout clothes that must have looked a lot better on the store mannequin, stood outside my car. "Luci!"

I opened the window and smiled, sweat forming from the effort. "Shari, how are you? How was your summer?"

"We've been going to the Hamptons every weekend while the kids are at camp. The usual. And you? How was *France?*" She put on her best affectation.

"Oh, you know, it was wonderful. Nothing like those habitual escapes, right?"

"Yep. You know exactly what you're getting. And *you* always get *France*. Lucky you."

"Yes." I wanted the conversation to be over.

"Well, now that you're back, you and Dalton will have to come over for dinner. Are you free this Saturday? Francine Clébert will be there with one of her fabulous desserts!" She practically sang the last line.

"Oh, really?"

"She's been dining with us a lot lately. Especially since Didier is off in God's country doing who-knows-what to save who-knows-who . . ."

"Right." I wanted to tell her he was most likely saving himself from her dinner parties. "Well, that sounds nice, but we'll have to pass for Saturday. We have a previous engagement. But thank you."

"Too bad. I'm sure Francine would like to see you, speak French and all that. Maybe next time?"

"Maybe next time. See you soon, Shari. My best to Jay and the kids." I started the ignition, imagining the look on Francine's face if I showed up at dinner, refusing to drink wine and recounting tales from the south of France, including a jarring bullfight I attended and the unexpected carnal response it drew from the crowd. I waved good-bye to Shari Miller like a torero retreating from his charge and headed straight home.

As I drove, I placed my hand on my belly, tempting communication with the teeny being inside me. Would it be another girl, like Jacqui? Or maybe a boy this time. I always thought a boy would be nice. They stick around and love their mothers. Girls fly away and get pregnant. Would he be a scholar, a risk-taker, a wanderer? Could he possibly ever find a way to disguise himself as an Ames? Or would Dalton have a question on his lips whenever he looked at the child or at me?

I removed my hand from my abdomen, not wanting to bond or inquire or dream. Not wishing to create an unstoppable curiosity about the person growing within me who could be the next president or find a cure for cancer or dance at the Bolshoi or be my best friend. Or be absolutely nothing at all.

The choice was all mine. Lucky me.

CHAPTER 37

Monday. The front door opened at eight AM and with it came the proverbial sounds of vacuum, broom, and sponge. Norma was here. It would be thorny seeing her again. And this time, I would have to let her go.

I took my time making my way downstairs. I was officially still on summer break. Jacqui was already seated in front of the TV with an empty cereal bowl watching a faded cartoon. I kissed her good morning.

"You know you're not supposed to eat in front of the TV."

Her sweet gaze was fixed on a big rooster on the screen. "You were sleeping and Norma said I could."

"Did she?"

"What's the big deal?" Jacqui had taken a more defiant tone lately. Most likely born of retaliation. I wondered how long it would last.

I continued into the kitchen to conjure up some breakfast and words—words about propriety for Norma. She had left the coffeemaker ready for me; all I had to do was turn it on. I quickly poured the grinds back in the container and dumped the water down the sink. As the hot water for my tea boiled, I heard a soft retching from the powder room. A moment later it repeated. I drew closer.

"Norma? Everything all right?" I knocked on the door.

A pause. Then fumbling. "Just a minute, Miss Luci."

I knocked again. There was no answer for a moment, and then suddenly Norma opened, looking pale and sickly. It took me aback.

"Nice to see you again, Miss Luci. Sorry, I'm not feeling so well."

"I can see that. Have you seen a doctor?"

"Yes. It's not contagious. Don't worry." She held her stomach in discomfort.

"Well, what is it? What can I get you?"

"Just give me a moment and it will pass. Maybe if you have some ginger ale, that could help." She tried hard not to look up at me.

Ginger ale? "Norma? Look at me."

She slowly tilted her pretty olive face toward the oncoming inquisition, appearing as if she were about to throw up again.

"Are you pregnant?" The words came out swiftly, tinged with judgment, and without an ounce of intended compassion. Just disbelief. And fear. Fear that maybe that dinner for two hadn't ended as I thought.

"Please, do you have any ginger ale? I feel sick again." She fell to a squat, throwing her head down between her knees.

I came back a moment later with a glass of soda. "It won't help much, but here."

She drank it in small, steady sips, eyes closed, looking like a child in the desert, not sure when she'd have her next drink.

"Norma, does your boyfriend know?"

"I don't have a boyfriend." She stared at the floor tiles.

"Are you going to keep the baby?" I had no right asking these questions, but I needed to know. I was beginning to feel ill myself. "Are you?"

She shook her head *no*, a tear forming in her eye. "I can't."

"It's okay. I'm sure you're making the right decision."

"I have no choice." She wiped the sadness from her wet cheeks.

I wanted to press her for more answers. An intense curiosity gnawed at me. I leaned on the doorjamb for balance and to calculate my next thought, next question. I subdued my own need to purge with a gulp of air. Could this be happening to both of us at the same time? What was the likelihood that it was Dalton's child? No relief came with that notion, just anger. Fury, in fact, that it was even a possibility. Were we all so much the same? I wanted to destroy any possibility of complicity. I dropped the bomb.

"Dalton and I will help you find a good clinic." An insincere, hypocritical hand landed on her shoulder.

"No! You cannot tell Mr. Dalton! Please! It is so embarrassing." A wild look took over her expression.

My own pulse shot up. "I understand. But eventually, Dalton will know." I bent down to meet her stare directly in the eye. "We tell each other everything." I lorded the false statement over her like a punishment. Like a terrible, cruel joke.

Yes, Dalton would know that I found out Norma was pregnant and that I helped her seek an abortion, and from his reaction I would see if it were his child or not. But could Dalton actually have slept with Norma? Was it even feasible? Or was it just demented wishful thinking, so that their actions would absolve me of my own? Time would tell. But for now, I was Norma's only ally and I needed to find the truth. Maybe the truth could set me free.

CHAPTER 38

"Why isn't the house clean?" Most men wouldn't notice the difference, but Dalton had an eye for the spotless.

"We had a little incident with Norma today."

"What happened?" A hint of annoyance rang in his tone.

"I found her throwing up in the bathroom, and thought it would be best to send her home."

"Was she all right?" He dropped his attaché on the seat next to the door with a *thud*.

"She will be. I'm taking her to a clinic tomorrow."

Hesitant. "Well, that's nice of you."

"You sound surprised."

"I thought Norma was still on your shit list, frankly."

"She can't ask anyone in her family to take her. She's too traumatized."

"Traumatized about being sick?" He squeezed his eyes at me as if trying to compute.

I lowered my voice. "Traumatized about being pregnant."

"What?" Dalton braced himself on the chair. "You can't be serious!"

"Quite serious."

"Norma's pregnant? God, I wonder—"

"—who the father is? She wouldn't say. Apparently, she doesn't have a boyfriend. Could be anyone." The last statement came out with a certain contempt and agenda.

Dalton looked even more riddled, empty of air or belief. "Anyone?"

"Either way, I'm the one who has to take her to the clinic."

"Wait." His voice went brittle. "Do you mean a medical practice or an abortion clinic?"

"She doesn't want to keep the baby."

Silence filled the room, palpable as any natural disaster.

"I can't believe it." The words came out as if he didn't intend for anyone to hear them.

"It happens every day. Especially with single women of her demographic." I sounded all the more cavalier, given my own circumstance.

He paused, lost in thought.

I watched him, questioning his innocence or guilt. "What are you thinking, Dalton?"

"Nothing. Just . . . forget it."

"Tell me."

"It's just that maybe there's another solution." He looked up at me, cautious.

"Norma's problem is not our problem." Defensiveness spiked in my tone.

"I know, but we do have a certain issue and this might help."

My stare gored into him, trying to read his words like a polygraph. "What exactly are you saying?"

"I know this may not sound rational, but hear me out. If you're open to it, maybe we can do a private adoption deal with Norma. You've been having such a hard time getting pregnant and this could be the gift that we've been waiting for."

"You think Norma's baby is our gift? Why would you think that?" My temper rose, each word held in a vise grip between clenched teeth.

"Because of the timing of it. And because we know her well and she would be giving the child a good home and be able to be a part of its life."

"A baby that she had with a perfect stranger? A baby whose DNA we'll never know? Did you even think for a moment that it might kill her to see the child growing up here? Or does your insane fantasy also include her co-parenting with us? Stopping by to clean the bathrooms and have a cup of tea? Are you fucking kidding me? What's the real reason you want this baby, Dalton? Why?"

A forced composure clamped his throat. "It just seemed like it could resolve everyone's problems, that's all."

"Really? Or would it just solve your problem?"

"How do you mean?"

"All I know is that while I was away, you two were having a cozy dinner together. So tell me, Dalton: Could this child possibly be yours?"

"What? You're crazy! I can't even talk to you when you're like this." An aggressive laugh slipped through his forced passivity.

I wanted him to burn alive. "Don't walk away! Answer me!"

"How could you accuse me of such a thing? What's wrong with you?"

"Maybe because you were so quick to want her baby. The whole point was to have a child of our own. Now you're ready to take anyone's kid!"

He calmed down in an instant, taking my hand in his before I lost my temper any further. "I'm sorry. You're right. It was a bad idea. Please forgive me and forget I ever said it. Our baby will be ours. Only ours."

The problem was, at that moment I didn't want a baby. Not ours, not Didier's, and definitely not Norma's. I just wanted my life back, unbound by lies and hypocrisy and doubt. Free of things I could never really be free of again.

Dalton held me tightly, tamping down his own unraveling.

The mood turned taciturn with nothing to soothe it or make it honest or whole again. I hadn't learned the truth. Maybe nothing had happened between Norma and Dalton. Or maybe they were as good at lying as I was. It was easy to see the world with suspect eyes—with the heart of a criminal waiting to be shackled.

Jacqui came bounding down the stairs, hearing unnaturally raised voices. "Is everything okay?"

It was the only question of the day. We would feign status quo for her sake.

"There's my princess . . ." Dalton held his arms out to her and she folded into them like two people sharing the same chromosomes. What more could he want?

CAFÉ ANTOINETTE

My eyes fell to the glass slipper on the mantel, recalling how Norma had wanted to try it on, while dreaming of a regal life—my life. Like so many things, that standing didn't quite fit me anymore. Neither did my image of loyal spouse and partner, or my hope of being a good mother and wife. Something had drastically shifted inside. A hostile takeover of the kingdom had occurred. And this final coup was making me sick to my stomach.

CHAPTER 39

She rang, choosing not to enter with her own key. Something kept her out. Perhaps shame. A whitewashed Norma stood on the stoop with her house key in hand. She was watery and broken. I invited her to step in but she wouldn't move, fettered by something I couldn't see and that rendered her immobile. Even her speech was manacled.

"Norma, please. Come in. I'll be ready in a moment. I called the clinic and they're expecting us. You have nothing to worry about." I urged her through the doorway, but she wouldn't budge.

"I can't. I won't." A super-storm of emotion formed between her small, honey-colored eyes.

"Have you changed your mind?" I tried to erase the alarm from my voice.

"I'm keeping it." She clutched at her belly as if to stop me from wrenching away her choice.

I paused. "Think, Norma. Are you ready to raise a child on your own with no one to help you or provide for you? I was a single mom for years, and it's harder than I can say."

"But then you found Mr. Dalton and he married you. So maybe that can happen to me."

Her mention of Dalton set me off. "It's not the same. You'll need to get your own life."

"Excuse me?" She took a step back.

"You can't just slide into my life when I'm not around. You can't try on my things or make claims to my husband." The words came out angry, un-buffered, accusatory, cruel.

Her liquid paleness turned icy. "Then you have nothing to worry about. I will keep my baby and stay far away from here. I don't need you and I don't need your husband. You didn't bring me here to help me, Miss Luci. You brought me here to get rid of my baby. Because you can't stand to see me have something you can't. Well, I'm sorry. There's nothing you can do about it." More words hinged on her lips, her tongue rolling over them, dousing the fire before it could ignite.

The house key was handed over with a furious, trembling hand.

I didn't call after her. I watched as she kept down the great heaving inside her—the wretched uncertainty and a baby too. A baby that might be Dalton's. A baby she'd keep.

First came relief. I wouldn't have to face the clinic, its antiseptic smells, heartbreaking faces, its self-righteous protestors with black shrouds and tortured signs. Perhaps I was as smug as they were, thinking that I could sway someone to do something out of guilt or morality—out of my own desire to keep things clean and tidy and in their natural order.

I suddenly felt heinous knowing that I was about to march a young woman to the gallows with sympathy that was meant to soothe my own soul, not hers. Hers be damned. I needed to save myself and my family. That was all that mattered.

The truth was that I didn't have the courage to make my own decision about the child growing inside of me. I wanted Norma to go first. To pave the way to loss. We both got pregnant without wanting it to happen.

Lots of women aborted for this reason alone: An unwanted child. Others did it because they couldn't afford it, or because they already had too many children and one more would compromise the lives of everyone. Some women lived with the hardship of having too many kids, some with the pain of termination, while others felt the emptiness of never having any at all. Everyone suffered losses, regrets. There was no right way.

Like so many, Dalton felt entitled to having children, as if they would somehow fill out his life. But what if not keeping a child was more loving and merciful than giving it an unwanted existence? When was enough really enough?

Dalton came home inquiring about my day at the clinic. I considered my options while picking at a stain on the counter. I could tell him that it all went fine. That Norma was on bed rest at home. That it was time for a change. That we could put the conversation to rest. My lies would stack up like cards on the table, ready to be knocked over at the slightest call on my bluff. But I couldn't.

"She changed her mind. She's going to keep the child. And she's not coming to work here anymore." My voice swept clean all concern.

Dalton poured himself a drink and fell noiselessly into his armchair. "Things are getting messier every day."

I looked at him, not knowing what he was referring to.

"We're going to have to find someone to clean all this up." He motioned to the house, but I felt he was pointing at me. He looked lost, holding onto a place that was no longer his to claim. It was true: Our lives had gotten terribly, irreversibly messy.

Guilt washed over me, making me feel even dirtier. I had caused Dalton to lose his luster. The dulled, victim-like look on his face said it all.

"Don't worry. I'll straighten it all up." I approached his chair, needing reconciliation. "Maybe there's something we can do to feel better in the meantime."

"What would that be?" He took a hard swallow, looking up.

"Let's go take a shower, then meet in bed."

"But your stomach virus . . . is it better?"

"Much better. Plus, I miss being with you, Dalt, and I'm ready to try again." There it was: the final whitewash of truth. Someone had to be lied to: Didier or Dalton. Someone had to be denied. The small, unwanted life taking root inside me needed to be accounted for.

He pulled me down onto his lap and kissed me deeply. I took it in, holding close what was truly mine.

"Come on. Let's go." I led him by the hand, finally ready to make his greatest wish come true.

CHAPTER 40

THE NEXT MORNING FELT almost normal. I bought into the falsehood I'd created. Dalton and I had made love the night before and were planning to do so again that night. I told him I was certain that the timing was right and that my month in France did me a world of good. I said all of this quite convincingly. So much so, I almost believed it myself. My words came as a balm to him, which only reinforced my investment. We were taking stock of our love again. This baby would heal us. I was doing this for us.

That's what I told myself: The secret life inside me would be my burden, my sacrifice, my gift to Dalton. Being with Didier had saved my marriage, not harmed it. I decided not to think about him anymore, or about possible paternity tests, or DNA, or any of the things that could confound or derail my newfound certitude.

Dalton handed me a cup of watered-down coffee with an unapologetic smile. I could issue no complaints. This was our life. He made me weak coffee every morning and I accepted it. These were the things we did for the people we loved.

Jacqui sat and drew pictures of pretty little girls with big eyes and giant flowers, the world enticing her with its amplified beauty once again. "Martin wants to take me on a drawing trip to the Central Park Zoo. We want to see the polar bears."

"I'm sure we can make that can happen, honey." I stroked her hair, thinking about caged animals and pretty little girls.

"Polar bears do not belong in New York City. Just like the French don't belong on the Upper West Side." Dalton spat the last statement into his cup, lips pursed with superiority.

"Lots of things don't belong in New York City. Like spiked heels, midwesterners, and baby strollers. But that's what makes it such an unexpectedly amazing place." I winked at Jacqui for collusion.

"The center of the goddamn world." Dalton flitted with sarcasm. "Excuse my French, Jacqui."

"I've heard worse." She focused on the daisies.

I froze. Did he know something about my day with Didier? "Actually, since the park is in the center of things, it's kind of fitting to fill it with zoo animals, if you ask me."

"But bad things happen when you take creatures from polar extremes and put them somewhere else." Dalton wagged his spoon for emphasis.

Lately, each statement seemed laced with innuendo. Eyes too wide. Words too precise.

The doorbell rang as he diluted his thought with a sip of coffee. "I'll get it."

Dalton came back into the kitchen a moment later with

apprehension drawn across his face like a Kabuki mask. Omar was standing by his side, looking creased and gray.

"Jacqui, can you go to your room for a few minutes. We need to talk with Mr. Omar."

Jacqui scooted away, leaving a trail of happy sketches behind her.

"Omar, what's going on?" I approached him slowly.

"It's Sabine . . ." He cupped his face in calloused, trembling hands.

"What's happened?"

"She's gone." The onslaught of emotion was unstoppable.

A sob rose up instantaneously, like I'd just witnessed someone getting run over by a truck. Dalton latched onto me and I let him.

"But I just spoke to her. She was tired, but not near dying. What happened, Omar?"

"The doctors wanted her to go another round with chemo and radiation. She'd had enough. You know Sabine. She wanted to do it her way. We had a beautiful, romantic evening together, and then she took the sleeping pills."

"*How could you let her do that?*" My words flew at him.

"I didn't. Had I known what she was planning, I would have fought her. She knew that. She did this all by herself."

His words hit me like a shock wave. Since when was overdosing on sleeping pills or keeping an illegitimate child really done for those we love? Weren't they more to spare ourselves any additional pain? My grief unleashed and I let Dalton soothe it as best he could.

"For you." Omar held out a bulging envelope. "She left this for you."

Inside, I found no apology, no explanation, barely a letter at all. Just a fragrant note sprayed with her signature perfume: *It was a damn good ride while it lasted; now it's your turn. Get a new lease on life. I know you'll do the right thing. Love you, girlfriend.*

Inside the envelope were the keys to Sabine's car—the Mercedes she'd won in her divorce. She always said a good car made a fine woman look finer. That car made her feel like she was going places, even if it were just down the street. It made her feel like a winner. This was her advice and final offering to me: Start again.

My best friend was gone in a puff of gardenia and every mile I'd travel would remind me of her iron will, her absolute drive, and her choice to die without a proper good-bye. Some things were too hard to understand. Some things we just did for those we loved.

Sabine was my polar extreme. We met in this suburban enclave where neither of us fit in. It was just somewhere in the middle. Perhaps Dalton was right: No good could come of creatures living where they shouldn't.

CHAPTER 41

New orleans jazz filled the hall where strange and familiar faces gathered, wanting to cry but unable to withhold their big watery, nostalgic grins. Sabine's coffin was carried through the hall as loudspeakers blasted "When The Saints Go Marchin' In." Clearly, this was part of her plan: a foot-stomping farewell, not a dirge. I wouldn't be surprised if she were buried in a tight, animal-print dress, a red push-up bra and a thong. I missed her so much, but her spirit was undeniably in the room, watching us all like a party planner from behind the wings. Her bitter ex-husband was even there, mopping tears in the back row like he'd been bumped from the front of the line.

The coffin arrived in front of the hall where dozens of wreaths with hot-pink roses were posing like a winner's circle. Satin messages curled around them with expressions of loss that somehow seemed misfit, given the buoyant feeling in the room. A striking black-and-white portrait of Sabine stood on an easel to the left. In it, she was pictured laughing, like someone had just told her the funniest thing she had ever heard. Something like, "Guess what? You're dead!"

Her head was tossed back gracefully, elongating her neck. Her lips parted, pulling her cheeks to perfect teeth-baring depths, and her eyes appeared half-closed as if through joyful exertion. I had seen her like this a million times, and yet this expression seemed entirely unexpected. It took us all off guard and no one could take their eyes off the image. It seemed to have nothing to do with the waxen, diminished person asleep in the coffin.

Sabine's eldest son, Ronald, got up to speak. Except he couldn't. His throat dried up, his eyes misted over, and the pale note he intended to read collapsed in his hand by his side. His brother Peter rushed up to buttress him, flattening the note down on the podium and reading a mere couple lines—more fortune cookie than farewell. Sabine had chosen brevity with those she held dear.

I noticed others clutching at pockets or rubbing small folded papers between fingers. Most everyone in the room had received a note from Sabine—just a simple, direct missive with no lingering sentiment. I reread my own and heard it like a cheer to keep me moving, living, driving. This was a genuine testament of love. Nothing maudlin or morose. Something we could keep in our pockets or next to our hearts and commit to memory, like a mantra.

One by one, people stood up in the hall and testified, speaking aloud the encouragements they'd received. Laughter echoed and sometimes tears. The scent of her fragrance filled the air. We breathed deeply, finding meaning in her words. I stood and delivered my message, dangling the car keys for punctuation. For entitlement. She was *my* best friend. As unlikely as our union seemed, we were given each other. And now I'd have to take the rest of the ride alone.

After the service, I approached Omar, who was bookended by Ronald and Peter in the receiving line. "Omar, everything was so beautifully *Sabine*. All of it."

"You were her closest friend, Luci. She thought the world of you."

"I thought the world of her too." My eye caught the picture. "Where did this come from?"

"Your friend, the photographer, took it. He knows how to capture the real essence of someone. The laugher and the suffering."

"Yes, he does." I considered how thoroughly he had captured me as well. I decided right then and there that I would have to contact him. I would let him know that Sabine had passed and that his portrait was perfect. I would withhold telling him the one true thing burning inside: a secret that my dearest friend took to the grave.

I touched the face on the picture, then held my hand to my stomach, wanting to give a blessing to my unborn child from her fairy godmother. My whole body shook. Dalton placed a quick hand on my shoulder to steady me.

"It's okay, sweetie. She's in a better place."

I resented his touch. I did everything not to brush him off or rail at him for not understanding the depth of my bereavement—for never recognizing anything but his own limited will. It was, after all, his constant yearning for a child that had made me stray. Expectation created nothing but pain. Why couldn't he leave well enough alone?

"Please . . ." The single word slipped through my teeth, seething, boiling down some other, truer sound. I wanted nothing more than to tuck myself in the luxurious car that was given to me and drive far, far away. To a better place, as Dalton would say. Except that I had no idea where in the world that might be.

CHAPTER 42

"I HEARD YOUR FRIEND DIED. I'M so sorry." Martin stood at the door of his small railroad flat, compassionate through a paucity of words.

"I guess Jacqui told you."

"She's worried about you. She says you haven't been yourself. I can see what she means. You look . . . different."

"It's just a hard transition. When someone dies, it makes you take stock of what's important . . . who's important. That's all."

"Yes, but there's something else. I've seen you look this way before."

I caught eyes with Martin. "I'm just really tired, Martin, and feeling down."

He held his tongue for a moment, still eyeing me. "Hmm. That must be it. Well then, come in. Jacqui's been working on a drawing in the kitchen."

I followed him to the tiny alcove. It was a slot, actually, with a kind of foldout stove that had to be raised in order for Martin to insert himself behind the counter. Jacqui was seated on a lonely stool coloring in her picture.

"Hi honey. What are you drawing? It's beautiful." I leaned down and kissed her on the head, taking in the strange, bulbous form she was creating.

She answered, not looking up. "It's a cocoon. The butterfly is in the chrysalis phase."

Martin's eyes opened wider as if in sudden realization. "Luci, there's something I need to show you in the other room. Let's allow the artist to finish her rendering."

I followed Martin into the living area, looking around for anything notable on display, but finding only the usual scarce furnishings and an odd collection of musical instruments. "What is it, Martin? A new oud?"

"No, it's the chrysalis phase! That's the look you have! I know it well. The swollen eyes and pale cheeks. You had it when you were expecting Jacqui. So, did Dalton finally get his wish? Are you pregnant?"

"Martin, lower your voice! Why would you guess something like that? I told you, I'm just tired and depressed because of Sabine."

"Well, how tired are you? When's the last time you had your period? You should check and see if I'm right. I have a feeling that I am!" He squinted as if sizing up the situation.

"We've been trying again, it's true. I might be, but I haven't tested yet." I hated lying to him. He could read me like a book.

"Well, you don't seem particularly excited about the possibility.

Things not going so well in paradise? Or are you still swooning over the puffed-up war photographer, what's-his-name?" Martin collapsed on the couch and waved a wooden flute at me like a pointer.

"Didier. His name is Didier. And things are fine between me and Dalt. Never been better, actually. Sorry to disappoint you."

"Oh, I'm not disappointed. Quite the contrary. I was worried you'd get involved with *monsieur* and make a mess of things. I know how wanton you can be with Frenchmen."

"Ha-ha." I kept standing as if on trial, trying not to show my discomfort.

"So, did you see this Didier character when you were there? I know you were planning on crossing paths." Martin's glare was growing more insidious, as if he were putting all the nasty pieces together in his head.

"Uh, yeah. We did, actually. We had a day of overlap when I first got there, before he took off for the Sudan."

"And . . . how did it go?" A reptilian smile emerged.

"What kind of question is that? We're friends, that's it."

"Except there you are, all alone in the south of France, in one of the most beautiful and romantic places on earth with some of the best wine and food and exceptional scenery. One could easily be tempted to misbehave." He was clearly enjoying the interrogation, taking advantage of the flute in his hands and making sudden snake-charming music.

"We had a lovely meal and went to a bullfight, and that's it." Sweat was beginning to form under my shirt.

"Did you say a bullfight? Really?" Martin leaned in, lowering his voice. "Okay, now I'm sure that you slept with him! People just don't go to bullfights in the south of France and walk away without a passionate roll in the hay. All that blood and seduction really get the heart pumping. I can tell you from my own experience."

"Well, your experience is not the same as mine!" I held my stomach.

"Are you sure? Because you look like you're about to throw up, which would just confirm my theory, except that it might change the issue of paternity. The papa, as opposed to the pupa." Martin seemed overly pleased with his pun and deduction.

"Martin . . . you've got a big imagination."

"Mama, look!" Jacqui entered the room with her finished drawing.

"Saved by the butterfly." Martin twirled his flute. "Jacqui, that's a beautiful picture. So much detail. You have the artist gene, for sure."

"Okay, kiddo, let's go before Martin takes credit for all your accomplishments, present and future."

"Let's just say I can't wait to see what else is born from this early stage of creation." He was talking to Jacqui, but looking straight at me.

"We'll be sure to keep you posted." I took Jacqui and her picture and headed out the door, realizing that it was only a matter of time before others would be able to break the code as well. Could I really do this to Dalton and live a life pretending that my child with another man was his? It seemed like the most unforgivable thing in the world. And yet, my only other choice was to terminate. Or was it?

CHAPTER 43

I HEADED OUT OF THE PHARmacy with a large bottle of B12 vitamin in hand, hoping it would curb my escalating nausea. Then I bumped into Shari Miller in the parking lot and wished I'd taken an immediate dose. Shari quickly mentioned that dinner parties were temporarily on hold due to the fact that she was busy redoing her bathrooms. In between re-this and re-that, she said words that I didn't comprehend. She said that Didier had already returned from the Sudan. He'd come back early. Something about an urgent situation. I asked if anything had happened to him.

She leaned in, making her expensive, musky fragrance fill the air and hasten my morning sickness. "It's some kind of family matter."

I could have swallowed the entire bottle of B12 at that moment and it would have done nothing to allay the unsettledness in my gut. What in the world had caused Didier to come back? Was he wounded in the field? I couldn't bear if something terrible had happened. Not now. Not after losing Sabine. Or maybe it was some complication at home. If anything had happened to Francine, Shari would have known about it. Most likely, the "family matter" concerned their marriage. Perhaps Francine had enough. Maybe she demanded Didier return home immediately and gave him an ultimatum. Surely, that's why he hadn't called me.

But I still wasn't sure if I should reach out. There was always the chance that he was as distraught as I was about our night together. Maybe I was the last person on earth he wanted to hear from. It was foolish to think otherwise. Telling him I was pregnant with his child would be insane. Completely disastrous. And it would only create more pain. The only thing to do was keep my absolute distance from Didier Clébert, though every cell of my body insisted on doing otherwise.

I said good-bye to Shari in a stupor, calculating my cool, not wanting to succumb publically to my rising anxiety. I sat in the steaming Mercedes for a moment, tapping the wheel and letting the burning, musty air and the scent of overheated groceries in the backseat fill my lungs. My legs stuck to the leather. My thoughts set a fire in my head. But there was no one to douse it out. No Sabine to speed-dial or rescue me. I was perfectly alone.

I considered driving to the cemetery. But Jacqui was expecting me back home. Life was expecting me back home. I had elected my role as wife and mother and I had no choice but to follow through. Who did I think I was? I was not free to make choices that would impact other people's lives like this. I had brought this whole stifling sequence of events upon myself. Boredom lured me there. Most people would do anything for the life I had. People like Norma. But I went ahead and ruined everything. I strayed from my path and now had to bear up to the consequences, living out the rest of my life on the loose footing of a lie.

Entering the house, I heard voices coming from the kitchen. I peeked around the doorway and saw Dalton seated close to Jacqui, holding her hand in between his and looking into her big eyes. He had fallen in love with Jacqui from the moment he met her. It was hard not to cave into her old soul. She was full of fair-minded thoughts and principled idealism. I wondered what she'd think of me now if she knew what I'd done.

"I used to want a little brother or sister, but I changed my mind. I like it this way. The three of us have fun together. If we had a baby, everything would change. Do you want everything to change?" Jacqui was always clear and resolute.

"It's not that I want our life to change. I love our life. I just think it would be even better with another family member, that's all. Remember? We all talked about this."

A grimace took over her face as she withdrew her hand from his. "Is it because you're not my real father?"

I stood quietly, stunned.

He swallowed hard, his face melting as it puddled in front of hers. "Jacqui, you know I think of you as my own. I always have. It's just that your mom and I have been married a while and it seems like the natural thing to do when you love someone. You have a child."

"But you already have me. Aren't I enough?"

I wished I'd been brave enough to say those same words to Dalton.

"Jacqui . . . please. Of course you're enough."

"Then?"

I noisily dropped my bag on the floor to announce my arrival, shouting *hello* from the next room. I couldn't bear another moment of my daughter's rising tide of emotions, the unanswerable questions, the same old responses filled with dispensations and a false view of fulfillment.

Dalton looked stricken as I entered the kitchen as though he had never truly considered Jacqui's right to vote and it was stinging him like an oversight on some final electoral tally. I gave Jacqui a squeeze and delivered a quiet kiss to Dalton's cheek. He looked up at me and forced a smile.

"Hey, guys. Anyone in the mood for spaghetti and meatballs? Because that's what I intend on making for dinner." I rubbed my hands together as if devising a secret plan.

"Mama, you know that's our favorite. You don't ever have to ask us that." Jacqui gave me that obvious look that preteen children often delivered, eyes rolling.

Dalton chimed in with a dramatically raised eyebrow and an exaggerated *"duh . . ."* that let the syllable ride out to ridiculous proportions.

The tension broke. Funny faces, favorite meals. I took on this role of wife and mother long ago and the truth was, I knew exactly how it had to be played out.

CHAPTER 44

I HAD READ THAT ASCORBIC ACID in vitamin C would do the trick, along with parsley and cohosh teas. And also aspirin. But if it didn't work after a month of trying, a clinic would be inevitable. It would be stressful inducing a miscarriage while also pretending to try and get pregnant with Dalton. Not to mention punishingly absurd. But it had to be done.

Plus, there was Didier. His presence was looming, even if I hadn't seen him. Just knowing he was back in town put all my senses on alert.

"Larry Klinger invited us over to barbeque this weekend. I said yes." Dalton tugged his tie with determination.

"You said yes? Without asking me first?"

"What's the big deal? I thought you'd like to see everyone. They've been asking for you. You've been so shut in lately. It'll be good for you to get out."

"If you recall, my best friend died. I'm not really in the mood for a party. And I don't want to see those people."

"*Those people* are your friends. They care about you."

"You go. I really have no interest."

"Go without you? What's wrong, Luci?"

"I just . . . I haven't been feeling well. Tell them that. They'll understand. I know that you enjoy your time with Larry and the guys, but I have absolutely nothing in common with their wives." It came out smug and superior, but I didn't care. Sitting around overstuffed patio furniture with thin conversation and weight-obsessed women was not what I needed.

Dalton felt my obstinacy. Instead of arguing, he put his arms around me. His practiced restraint and concern came delivered two inches from my face. "Look, I know you're still sad about Sabine. I am too. But of all people, she would want you to get out and have fun."

"Exactly. And those people are no fun." I dug my fists into his pockets, not willing to surrender.

Dalton's displeasure was visible, as if someone had just scuffed the high shine on his wing tips. "All right, then. I'll cook up a lie and tell them we can't make it."

As he withdrew from my grip, I felt a small piece of paper in his pocket and pinched it between my fingers.

His eyes widened as I pulled it out to examine. "Give me that."

"What is it? A phone number some shameless customer slipped you? It wouldn't be the first time." I turned away, smirking while I unfolded the paper. But it was not a phone number. It was a receipt.

"A little premature to buy a baby stroller, wouldn't you say?"

He loosened the choke hold on his tie. "It was a gift. That's all. A gift. From both of us."

"From both of us to whom?" But I knew it before he said the name. "You bought this for *her*?"

"Why say it like that?"

"Are you kidding me, Dalt? Were you even planning on telling me about this gift of ours?"

"Please don't get all worked up about it. It was the right thing to do."

"Why is that?" I paced the room looking for steady ground, but the floor was quicksand.

"Because Norma worked for us a very long time. And now she's got no steady job and is expecting a child. Plus, the way you let her go wasn't exactly kind."

"She said that? You've been talking to her? I can't believe this!" But I could. Did I really think that I was the only one guarding secrets?

"I was simply concerned for her. She's having a baby and she's got absolutely no one."

"Well, apparently she's got you, and right where she wants you. What a conniving bitch."

"What the hell?" Dalton looked at me as if I'd knocked over a disabled person to secure my place in line.

"That's what I should be asking *you*, Dalton. What the hell were you doing with her? For once and for all, just tell me!"

He held something more than his breath before speaking. "Is that what you think? I show a little kindness toward a sweet, young person who's worked with us for years, and suddenly I've knocked her up? You're ridiculous and jealous, and you're way out of line, Luci."

"Screw you! I'm not jealous of that stupid, manipulative girl who fawned all over you every chance she got. Who's ridiculous, Dalton? Me or you? You actually fell for her ploy. I'll bet she'll make you godfather just to have your expensive gifts keep her afloat."

"Stop talking." His manicured hand jutted out like a shield.

"I won't stop talking. Not until you tell me the truth: *Did you or did you not fuck her?*"

My voice hissed to suppress an internal scream. It was an ugly sound that wanted to admit to everything—to betrayal and revenge and rupture. It was a squelched cry meant to travel across Scarsdale and pierce through the etched glass doors of Café Antoinette, hurtling into the ears of Didier Clébert with deafening urgency.

"I will not dignify that with a response." Sweat was forming, his throat turning red and pulsing, almost reptilian.

"Fine! You can have Norma and her bastard child, because it seems that's the only baby you're going to get!" I slammed a drawer as hard as I could, jolting a lamp to the ground and shattering it to pieces.

A moment later, Jacqui rushed into the room, eyes wide. "Is everything all right, Mama?"

I leaned on the dresser, suddenly feeling dizzy, sick, about to faint, my feet pooled in colored shards. "It's fine. Go back to your room."

"But Mama—"

"Just go!" Impatience cut through my voice like broken glass.

Jacqui pointed to my thigh where blood was spreading into the fabric of my pants. "You're bleeding. . . ."

CHAPTER 45

THE EMERGENCY ROOM WAS half empty. Dalton and Jacqui filled it with anxiety. A nurse came for me in a wheelchair while Dalton filled in papers and Jacqui clenched my hand. I was wheeled back to a small room and made to lie down. The room was beige and sanitized with a stack of rubber gloves, masks, and tissues on the counter. I remembered the days when doctors used bare hands. But times had changed. We were all protecting ourselves against something: infection; heartbreak. All of it.

An older doctor walked in and greeted me with a limp, moist grip. His features were crooked and pallid to distraction. I couldn't help but focus on his imperfections—the tiny clusters of dried white spit caked up in the corners of his mouth; the thick, discolored whiskers hanging on his lip like palm fronds over a decaying *palapa* hut.

His big, ochre-colored teeth issued a slightly protruded "Hello...."

"Hello." I slipped deeper into the bed, considering my own image. Every part of me lay prim and still and covered in blood. "Doctor, there's something you should know. I'm several weeks pregnant. My husband doesn't know about it. It was still too early and I was waiting to tell him . . . to be sure. The news will break his heart." Tears summoned to the surface.

"I'll do an ultrasound right now."

The nurse, portly, efficient, lost in middle age, placed a white paper gown over my torso. A blast of shiny white light ignited above, making her appear to have a halo. She looked softer, younger, more alien.

The doctor covered his questionable smile with a pale blue surgical mask. Better, I thought. I liked the blue. Except I couldn't help thinking that the blue of his mask and the yellow of his teeth would make green. Green things popped to mind: Shari Miller's lawn, Jacqui's drawing of a cocoon, salads with Sabine.

As the doctor gently placed the probe into my uterus, his assistant stood by like an insurance policy. I could suddenly see for the first time an image of what was inside me and uttered a silent prayer.

It didn't take long for the doctor's pronouncement. "I'm sorry, Mrs. Ames. You've suffered a miscarriage. We'll do an immediate DNC and remove what remains of the fetus."

I nodded in disbelief, tears blocking my view of the darkening screen. This child I had never wanted was no longer an option, nor a threat, nor a promise. It must have sensed my plans to flush it out with herbs and teas and done me the favor of vacating all on its own. But suddenly, I wished it hadn't left me with no choice.

The nurse wheeled me into an operating room where an anesthesiologist was waiting. She drew the curtain as the doctor reviewed my chart. "Have you ever had general anesthesia before?"

"Yes, once."

"Good. So just relax while we put the mask on you. You won't feel a thing."

Not feeling a thing seemed perfectly welcome and yet wholly impossible. I immediately sensed its effect as the gas started wafting in. It reminded me of college days, smoking hash, then falling asleep to dreams that were so vivid and surreal.

"Luci? How many fingers am I holding up?" The nurse was a big, blurry white cloud above me.

"Uhhh . . . four. Four, right?" It looked like four but I couldn't be certain.

"And now?" She held up another configuration of digits, but it all seemed the same.

"Don't know . . ." My eyelids were closing, drawn together by a magnetic force. I wanted nothing more than to sleep a deep sleep and wake up a different person in a whole new life. Someone who didn't lie and cheat and miscarry.

The doctor lifted his mask and leaned in. His teeth grew closer as he approached earshot and spoke softly. "Luci, can you still hear me?"

"The baby . . ." The dream was coming fast. So bizarre. Just like college. Didier and I were holding hands in the park, taking pictures, drinking wine, a bassinette on the blanket.

"It's going to be all right, Luci." Someone patted my hand.

"Please don't tell Didier about the baby."

"Do you mean the father?" Alien eyes grew wide.

"Yes . . ." And suddenly, everything went green, green, green; like a carpet of grass and a baby caterpillar. I was out like a light.

CHAPTER 46

I SAT IN THE RECOVERY ROOM IN a daze. Dalton hovered beside me, as polished and fragrant as a groomsman. Though silent, he seemed to echo the throbbing emptiness inside me where something full and alive used to be. The evacuation felt like a vaguely absent memory, except that the pain was worsening by the moment.

"The doctor told me." Dalton held my hand with no feeling, no pulse.

"Where's Jacqui?"

"The Constantins came for her. She's worried about you."

"I'll be fine."

"So, did you know?" He stared at the floor as if his peace of mind laid trampled on it.

I looked up questioningly, as if I needed further prompting. Buying time.

"Did you know that you were pregnant?"

"I didn't want to get your hopes up . . . in case something like this happened." And there it was: The final lie swept under the rug.

"How many weeks along were you?"

"I can't talk about it right now. Okay?" Tears welled up on cue.

"I'm sorry. For everything. It's been too much pressure. For you, for me, for Jacqui. She doesn't even want a sibling anymore. I pushed too hard."

I nodded, wanting him to feel badly, to hand over my guilt to him and exonerate myself.

The door opened and the doctor came in. "How are we doing?"

"The pain is getting worse."

"That's normal. You can take these pills every few hours for the first couple of days until it subsides." He handed me a small container. "You're free to go as soon as you're feeling ready."

Dalton extended his hand. "Thank you, Doctor."

"You're quite welcome, Didier. Luci, please call me if you need anything."

Dalton withdrew his hand and took a step back. "My name is Dalton."

"I'm so sorry. My mistake." The doctor looked at me as if cracking some code, then left the room hiding his horrible smile.

A man with big teeth who would come to know my secrets. There it was. Just as the gypsy had said it would be. A chill drew up my spine.

Dalton stared through me. "Why in the world would he call me Didier? What's that about?"

"I have no idea. I'm ready to go now." I reached for his hand.

We left the hospital in silence, calculating harsh words, broken things, a bloodied baby, a slip of the tongue. All evidence was destroyed, but Dalton was still doing the math.

The next days passed in tomblike quiet, buried in discomfort and contemplation. I obscured myself under covers and pillows and numbed the pain with medication. Jacqui stayed close by, concerned, never having seen me like this before. I couldn't reassure her. The void growing between me and the world was as vast as the distance between Scarsdale and St. Rémy. In desperation, Jacqui called Martin. He came by to cheer us up with light music and conversation. It made Jacqui feel better to have him there, so I encouraged his visits. He made her smile and fixed me teas.

"Whatever you need," he told me over and over. He meant it. Where Martin failed as a partner, he made up for as a friend.

Dalton went through the motions: Coming home early from work to check on me and take charge of domestic tasks. He tended to the basics, but no more. Requisite care. Out of guilt or retribution or betrayal, I couldn't tell. And I didn't care. After a great natural disaster, I didn't think that life could ever go back to the way it was. And maybe it shouldn't.

On my first day out of bed, I picked up the phone and called the university, exaggerating my condition to the department head and requesting a medical leave for the upcoming semester. "Complications," I said. There had been an urgent surgery with complications. No elaboration was necessary.

Then I got into my car and, with the scent and willpower of Sabine to accompany me, drove.

CHAPTER 47

An indescribable need for obscurity consoled me and kept me on the road with no destination. It was something I'd always done in my single years: Wander off. It did me good to be anonymous and adrift. Scarsdale suddenly felt as lonesome and unknown as anywhere on the planet. I could somehow imagine the ruins inside its grand old homes and forget about my own. In the past, I'd always gone to places like Greece for the myths and empty shores, the secluded swims and silent hikes where the only sound was the *thwack* of squid being beaten tender against the rocks—a sound that ticked away the hours like an accusing eight-handed clock. Time was more allegorical then. Less painfully accurate.

Back then, I'd plan nothing more than bathing topless during the afternoons and dancing recklessly into the nights. I had weathered enough guilt and incense in the northern countries. What appealed to me was a space without monuments or memories. A place without temptation. Gavdos was like that.

I'd first noticed it depicted on a menu place mat in a local taverna in Crete. The hand-drawn map showed a small brown speck in a big blue sea at the southernmost point of Greece. It was the final dot in the ellipsis where Europe quietly ended in a trail of unknown islands and the earth gave into the loud punctuations of North Africa. I had never seen this tiny island before, obviously an oversight with most cartographers and place mat illustrators. But I was always pulled toward things that were left unnoticed, easily obscured by a gravy stain or a wine spill.

I asked the taverna owner, who drowned out every dish he served with heavy doses of French cologne, to tell me more about the speck.

"Gavdos?" he said, forcing his eyebrows together in a long question mark. "No food, no water, no people, no discos. No good."

I could certainly live without the people and the discos. I started filling in the empty calendar spaces of my mind with Gavdos.

I showed up at the harbor early the following morning and noticed a wind-battered sea captain straddling a ramshackle dock like a piece of conquered land and yelling orders to a couple of toothless sailors. The men hastened their pace and loaded up the small boat with coffee and fruit, flatbread and cloudy bottles of ouzo. A week's worth of supplies would wobble their way to Gavdos, and apparently, so would I. I stepped onto the dock like a shaky piece of inventory.

The captain thrust eight crabby fingers into my face and repeated *"eyit"* to make sure I knew that he wouldn't be back for a good number of days. I handed him a few moist bills for the ride. He handed me a cup of molten-thick coffee, gesturing for me to drink it before the boat lurched out to sea.

We bobbed along for the first hour—me holding my stomach and focusing on an area of chipped paint that didn't seem to move as much as the rest of the vessel. The remainder of the time I fought off dizziness and heaves, and imagined what a stable life and fixed job would feel like.

When I finally disembarked with the boxes of booze and bread, I encountered a land so barren, so arid that I knew nothing but sad stories could grow there. Only a handful of people lived on the island and they all seemed to endure on a steady diet of pet chickens, old goats, and memory.

There was no official place to stay on Gavdos, just an empty post office in the middle of the island with a few iron cots available at fifty cents a night. I had often fantasized about staying overnight in a department store, slipping on layers of silk pajamas and rolling around Barcaloungers. Or even being locked in a toy store and fashioning a mattress out of stuffed animals. But I never imagined sleeping in the cold, dark interior of an abandoned Greek post office with an old mailbag for a blanket and a yellowed envelope under my head. I decided to lodge under the stars instead, borrowing a cover off the local woman from the fish shack.

I woke the first morning to the early buzz of flies at daybreak and to the smell of fried eggs at the shack. In eight days, I figured I'd develop an unusual taste for fried food and a deep hatred for flies. Although, I questioned if it might turn out the other way around. As

I watched the handsome woman fix my breakfast, I thought about destinies and lifetimes, and what made some of us choose lost little, inconvenient islands while others opted for Manhattan.

I headed out for the far reaches of the craggy eastern shore not looking for anything in particular, just a feeling of sovereignty and a sense that I could survive by myself. I didn't want anything at all to burden my experience except the half-liter of water that I carried. It was what I had been waiting for: the perfect isolation, the brief whitewash of time. Just me on every horizon. The beating shoreline kept time with my step and I walked for a long while following its meter, ignorant of the passage of hours. My thoughts rushed in as fast as the waves, but got sucked away with each new tidal pull.

My skin had already turned a blackish-brown from so many weeks of sun, and the wind was blowing a fresh layer of sea salt on my body that gave it a look of lace and ash. My faded pink cotton shirt was sticking to me like raw flesh and I could feel small pools of sweat forming under my breasts.

Maybe it was the feeling of being profoundly alone, but I was relieved when finally all of my clothes came off and I was free to roam naked over the earth. It was strange to be so entirely exposed and yet remain so totally unseen. Like a spirit, I thought, and wished I could take a picture of myself in this place to always remember what it felt like to be alive and invisible.

It was either the constant push of the wind or the fact that I had neglected to bring enough drinking water that started to wear me down. A flat rock looked like it offered a good opportunity to take a rest. Its surface was hot and sharp against my spine and I laid my clothes on top of it to thinly buffer myself against its edges. And though there was no shelter from the blazing sun, the flies were no longer apparent.

I don't know how long I drifted off, splayed on the rock like some beatnik sacrifice. Crevasses began to form on the soft part of my back and legs and the fleshy part under my arms. I'd become branded by the rock and yet slept as deeply as a baby on a feather bed. I snuggled under a blanket of sun while the wind blew as comforting as a mother's lips across a child's wound.

The sounds of distant bells floated across the hot air and woke me from my sleep. Before I even opened my eyes, I felt a presence. Maybe a goatherd had found me there, naked, and watched me at a close distance. Whatever it was, I sensed that I was not alone. I could discern a man leaning over me, as if he could reach over and touch me if he wanted to. But what I saw when I opened my eyes was even more alarming.

There he was, just as I had imagined him, standing only a few feet away and looking right through me as if beckoning my soul to come alive. My heart raced into my throat and choked back a scream. Any sound would fall silent in this place. I quickly sat up to shelter my body against an attack, but he didn't move. Rather, he quietly summoned me over to him. Before I could respond, he was gone, obliterated in a burst of sun and air.

I arrived at the fish shack at nightfall, eight long hours after my departure. *"Eyit"* I heard myself repeating as I stood parched and besieged by gadflies. The owner had apparently spent the latter part of the day with worry beads, concerned about where the American vagabond went and what she had gotten into. She sat me down to an offering of figs and yogurt and drew a map of the island on a napkin.

A small group of curious villagers gathered and, as everyone slipped happily into paint-thinning mixtures of ouzo and ginger ale, I indicated to them as best I could how far I had gone along the shore. The woman traced her finger over the map-napkin and slowly began to speak, unraveling a story that her grandmother used to tell her about Theseus and the souls of warriors that inhabited the distant reaches of the island. The others sat quietly and listened. It was a story they all knew by heart.

A Danish traveler also listened, wearing an ironic northern smile of superiority and disbelief, as if hearing a childish spook story told around an innocent fire. I wanted to join in his amusement, but what I had seen and felt on the beach that day seemed too real. As I told the villagers what I'd experienced, they responded with unflinching, silent nods.

The Dane set out the next day with camping gear and four liters of water. He would follow the napkin to the point I marked along the eastern shore and come back with a souvenir or a ghost story. He wanted to hear the goat bells and go face-to-face with a great warrior God. He wanted Theseus—the Ride. It was sometimes like that for travelers: They needed to capture a meaningful encounter and put it in their pocket. But meaningful encounters, like ghosts, never came when you looked for them. They had to look for you. All you could do was show up and surrender.

I glimpsed my worn-out face in the rearview mirror. Years without true adventure had become evidence on the pale surface of my skin. The painkillers had run out, the back roads started to seem all too familiar, and for the first time, tears were an impasse. I could no longer see anybody else's tragedy, just my own.

One thing was for sure: Each place had a way of leaving its mark. Gavdos would remind me of losing myself to erratic roving and mythic adventure. Scarsdale would never let me forget that a little being was also lost in some fickle place inside me. An innocent victim was caught in the crossfire of my disingenuous life. The question was, If I could go back in time, would I have done anything differently? Wasn't I lucky to be saved by divine intervention? The problem was, I wasn't feeling saved or lucky at all. Just doomed to receive more visits from unwelcome ghosts and to wander the world waiting for my misplaced soul to finally come alive.

CHAPTER 48

"LUCI? *C'EST TOI?*" HIS VOICE CUT across the florescent-lit pharmacy aisle like a mistral wind in the southern French plains.

I looked up, not believing it possible. "Didier. You're here?" He appeared like a familiar face from a dream.

He approached cautiously, leaning in for a kiss on the cheek, but noticing my delicate state. "Are you okay?"

"I'll be fine. Why are you here?" There was an unintended chill to my tone.

"Annual flu shots. It's that time." He pointed to the pharmacy sign and an obvious grin crept across his face.

"No, why are you back in New York already?"

He laughed, softening into boyishness. It was a look that rendered him even more striking. "Luci, I wanted to call you. I really did. I'm sorry. Forgive me. But things accelerated so quickly and well—the most wonderful, miraculous thing happened in the Sudan. And when it did, I needed to come back immediately. I'm sure you'll understand once I tell you."

"Okay, then. Tell me. What happened?"

As Didier prepared to fill me in, another sound wafted down the vitamin aisle: a clicking of low heels. Up clacked Francine holding hands with a little black boy, eyes big and glassy. He gripped her finger tightly, still uncertain of his steps. Didier raced over to pick him up, kissing him on the head and speaking to him in a soothing tone. Francine looked as unpleasantly amazed to see me as I was to see her. We offered one another polite nods of recognition, though it was clear from her darted glances back and forth between the two of us that she still questioned Didier's intentions. Unfortunately, the truth she was looking for could only be found in hospital hazmats bins and in the phantom swell of my tender abdomen.

Didier brought the boy close to me. He looked coyly into my eyes and then buried his face in Didier's shirt. "Don't be shy. This is my friend, Luci. And Luci, I am so happy to introduce you to the newest member of our family. His name is Zareb. It's a long story, but I had the opportunity to adopt him from an orphanage and I jumped at the chance. He is our dream come true. Right, Francine?" Didier turned to his wife, who was quietly analyzing the situation and clearly feeling the victor.

"We have never been happier, it's true." She kissed Zareb's little hand and all her usual rigidity and acrimony melted like frosting in the sun. Motherhood had been missing from her recipe book all this time, and its sudden appearance rendered her doughier.

I was speechless. Didier and Francine had a son. He had done what he'd always wanted: Spare the life of one child from war. He had saved a little human being. I knew he could salvage no more. I placed my hand on my stomach and held it there, balancing myself.

"Congratulations to you both. He's absolutely beautiful."

A strange silence mixed with loss and gain filled the medicine-tainted air. "So, does Zareb have his first flu shot today?" I tried to make light conversation with Francine.

"Yes, he does. And so does his daddy. Both of my sweet boys had to come in." Francine was already playing up her new role. Any moment now, she'd refer to herself in the third person.

"I'll take the little boy first." The pharmacist approached us with an invitation to follow.

"I'll go with him." Francine took the child by the hand and nodded good-bye to me, triumphant.

Once they left the aisle, I stared in Didier's eyes. I remembered the last time I'd seen them so close, our indelible night of passion and all the life and miles that had transpired since then. I looked at him knowing that I had been carrying his baby inside me, and that I had lost it.

"Are you sure you're okay, Luci? You don't seem yourself."

"Just a recent health setback. Something I picked up in France."

"Well, I hope you recover quickly." He couldn't grasp the full import of those words.

How can someone who's been fantasized over, dreamed about, shared intimacies with at the deepest level, suddenly become a stranger in less than two months? I felt my desire and vulnerability shutting off like a valve that had been left dripping for too long. Wrenched closed. It was the same mechanics that had been happening between me and Dalton. I looked at Didier as if I barely knew him.

"I want you to know that witnessing your relationship with Jacqui really inspired me. *You* inspire me, Luci." He took a step closer, wanting to clasp hands, but I tucked mine away for protection. "And I'll always keep the memory of St. Rémy with me. It was truly special, but *hélas* . . ."

A dull throb was taking over my gut. There would be not enough painkiller on the shelves for this moment. I rallied whatever shreds of strength and dignity I had left. Pain was my driver.

"You know what, Didier?"

He looked at me tenderly.

"You're full of shit."

"Excuse me?" He squinted at my lips, as if I wasn't speaking the same language.

"It's all just a game for you. You traipse around the world looking to save yourself from boredom. You have affairs, jet off to wars, rescue a child. It's just a regular day at the office for you. Except there are never any actual consequences. Do you even think about what you're doing or who you hurt along the way? I don't think you do. But I'll tell you this: To be a parent, you'll need to put your ego aside and take responsibility for the crap you pull. You, Didier Clébert, do *not* inspire me. You disgust me." My words slashed across him, leaving switchblade marks on his expression.

The pharmacist came back, suddenly interrupting Didier's oncoming excuses, his retreat. And as this strange man who had once been my lover skulked away, he stole a glance back—his face seeming sadder, revealing some misplaced conviction with nowhere to go.

I didn't care.

Didier Clébert entered the small area set aside for inoculations.

CAFÉ ANTOINETTE

There would be no anesthesia, no counting backwards, no accidental testimonials of what had transpired. He could keep all of his secrets and, with the small prick of a needle, walk away. Immunized.

CHAPTER 49

"Thanks for driving me to the city today, Mama. It's better than taking the train." Jacqui laid her mildly damp hand on mine as I gripped the steering wheel.

"My pleasure. Plus, I want to see Martin."

"Can I ask you something?" She adjusted in her seat, mustering the query. "You and Martin are like best friends. Why didn't you stay together?"

"I guess you have the right to ask that." I considered my daughter's innocence and hoped my past wouldn't skew her future. "Well, we were young and I suppose not mature enough to make that kind of commitment to each other. Being married and raising a child is a big deal. It changes everything."

"In a good way?"

"In a very good way, but you have to be ready for it."

"So, you were ready with Daddy?"

"I was. And he was a really good father to you." Everything about Dalton was already coming out past tense.

"I know. Except now he wants another baby and I don't. Do you think you guys will have one?"

"I don't think you have to worry about that." I clasped the wheel and tried not to let on that I'd been losing my grip since the conversation started.

"Mama, can we stop at the French bakery? I want to get Martin some madeleines. He loves them."

"Okay, sweetie. How about I give you the money and you run in. I'll wait outside and make a call." I still couldn't step foot in Café Antoinette.

I didn't have to.

Within the first minute, Francine was dangling in front of me like a ripe fruit from a tree.

"*Salut.* Your daughter told me you were waiting outside . . . making a call?" She indicated the lack of a phone in my hand.

"It ended quickly."

"I see." Her expression shifted from spurious to guarded. "Luci, there's no need to pretend. I know that you saw Didier this summer, even though you promised to keep away from him."

"Francine, I saw him as a friend." The lie even seemed transparent to me.

"A friend? Did he take you to his favorite bistro and order his favorite paté? Did you drink wine and wander the streets, perhaps take in a bullfight?" Her questions were filled with the rancor of the obvious, not of the betrayed.

"What's your point, Francine?"

"You understand nothing. This is just something that he does. He's a man. He needs escapes. But he always comes back to me. Always."

"I don't know what you're talking about."

"I think you do." Francine pointed to my beaded necklace. The one Didier had bought me in St. Rémy. Then she revealed an identical one from under her blouse.

My heartbeat quickened. I flushed under the threat of more questions.

"All men have weaknesses. It's just that some have better taste than others." She was aiming her comment at me and not the cheap necklace.

There it was. I could pretend no longer. There was nothing more to lose. "Then why do you put up with it?"

"Why? Because nothing is perfect." She flipped her short, clipped hair back in rebellion.

"Funny, I thought you were all about perfection."

"My *work* is all about perfection. But love and marriage, those things are always imperfect. It's very hard to find an independent, intelligent man who allows my career to be the primary focus in the marriage. I can live with Didier's transgressions. They mean nothing. In the end, he gives me what I want and I give him what he needs."

"And what would that be?"

"A long leash."

"Maybe Darfur was a little too long for you this time." I was feeling snide, bulletproof.

"What does it matter now? Like I said, he came back. And with a son. He won't be going on any more silly adventures for a long time. But what I said before still stands: Stay away from him."

Francine could have never divined how far away I wanted to be. Even so, the anger I felt wasn't totally directly toward Didier. He hadn't been lying to me or betraying anyone. He was simply being true to himself. Cheating on his wife was something he did with apparent frequency and Francine turned a blind eye. Because of this freedom, he probably felt indebted to stay with her. For them, it was a win-win. I was the only loser. The beads around my neck were suddenly as heavy as a noose, while Francine's shone like a jeweled collar on a favorite pet.

Jacqui walked out of the bakery with a big smile and a small bag of buttery sponge cookies. But there was nothing at all to absorb the infinitely bitter taste in my mouth.

CHAPTER 50

THE MANHATTAN SKYLINE stretched out like a power cord. It pulsed and surged with brick-and-mortar potential. The late-summer air was rancid smelling, as confidant and enticing as any wrongdoing. Little more than twenty miles to the north stood the flawless facades of the suburbs where the white-washed days stretched into sunny, entitled tedium, and people tucked in for the night with devious thoughts lurking in polished cotton.

I was still coming to terms with my own tainted deeds and bad smells. I rightfully owned them all. My freewill had exercised them into being. I had strayed in my marriage—a union that was now kept intact through vague compromise and blurred lines. Secrets always had a way of showing up and tearing into flesh.

The truth was, I didn't trust Dalton. I still questioned his fidelity, though nothing but instinct and DNA would ever prove it. Either way, there was no need to arm myself with more excuses. No reason to vent. Staying together would mean spending the rest of our days in the crucible of our privileged setting, watching Jacqui grow and our lives unfold into something enriched and routine. Things would go back to normal and the artifice of normal would have to suffice.

"You're awfully introspective today." Martin passed me the plate of madeleines.

I waved them away. "I was just thinking how nice it is to be in the city again."

Jacqui reached for a third cookie and I blocked her hand, not wishing my daughter to acquire a taste for Francine's perfectly delusional recipes.

"Well, you should come more often. I swear, you people who move to the country forget about sophistication and spend all your time thinking about car washes and composting."

"We live in the suburbs, not the country, Martin."

"That's even worse. A purgatory of not being one thing or another . . . a completely false construct. Like polyester."

Jacqui laughed. "That would be a good name for a dog."

He bandied around other pet names like Teflon and Nylon just to keep Jacqui in giggles.

"The point is, unless you want this fine young girl to become a topiary artist, she should be spending more time in the city." Martin looked at Jacqui for approval.

"I'm not opposed to the idea." I hid a percolating thought behind my coffee cup.

Jacqui looked up at me. So did Martin.

"The problem is," I continued, "that you don't have room for her here. And you certainly don't have room for me. And I might be needing some more time in the city too."

Martin understood without me saying anything more. He could see the outline of my precipice. My desire to jump. He led the way. "Well then, I may have just the solution." He was on his feet, grabbing keys and slipping into sandals. "Follow me. I have to show you both something. This is too perfect!"

Without question, Jacqui and I joined hands and followed Martin out of his studio and up the elevator to the top floor of the building. He opened the door to one of the apartments.

"Whose place is this?" Jacqui asked first.

"It belongs to my friend, Sharon. She's out of town and I'm watering the plants while she's away."

"Is that what we came to do? Water her plants?" I took in the sunny flat, its windowsill of greenery framing views of the Upper West Side and a battlefield of rooftop water towers.

"No, I already did that this morning." Martin was beaming with excitement. "Sharon has the flat up for sublet. I'm looking after it until it rents. Isn't it fantastic? And it comes completely furnished." Martin could never quite grasp how people made lifetime commitments to furniture, homes, or other people.

"A sublet . . . really?" I inspected the place more closely. "I could get used to this kind of view every morning."

"Mama, you'd move here?" Jacqui's voice sounded with reticent alarm.

"I'm just saying it's very nice. What do you think?"

"We can't just leave home! What about Daddy and school and your job?"

"Well, honestly, all those things are very close by. Wouldn't it be an adventure spending the school year in the city? You could even enroll at the French Academy. I have very good connections there." The budding idea was washing over me like a wave of warm seawater, glistening with micro-life and possibility.

Jacqui was still in the parenthesis of youth, uncertain how words and commitments could either bind her or get her rolling into a subsequent ellipsis.

"So, we could rent it and live in the same building as you?" Jacqui pointed at Martin, beginning to see the light.

"That's right! But you haven't seen the best part yet. Follow me." Martin led us to the master bedroom. Windows spread across two walls forming a perfect, angled panorama of the city, sparkling like Oz. "Scenery like this doesn't come easy in Manhattan."

"Look at the park, Mama!" Jacqui was already glued to the pane, an alien looking down from the mother ship at the land about to be conquered, the new creatures to be encountered.

"I'm looking." And I was. It was a view I had seen before, but from a different perspective.

Martin pointed to an open space in the park. "That's north meadow field, Jacqui. We've gone walking there."

"I remember!" Jacqui was already reclaiming lost terrain, distant in memory and birthright.

I remembered too. North meadow field. *The center of the center of the universe.* The very epicenter of Manhattan. And it was being offered to me. Again. I couldn't help but laugh.

"What's so funny?" Martin was already smiling.

"I like it."

"I like it too." Jacqui squeezed my hand and it was the first time I could feel a pulse return to my body, my blood.

"Shall I call Sharon and tell her I found a nice family to sublet the place?" Martin winked as if daring me.

I looked at Jacqui who was making small, vigorous, involuntary nods, eyes wide. "Yes, Martin," I countered. "Why don't you make that call right away."

The three of us stood like mountaineers on the verge of some great crag. Emboldened. Unstoppable. Ready to surmount anything.

CHAPTER 51

Not long after Jacqui and I made our move into the city, Dalton filed for divorce. I didn't resist. When I stopped by his store to drop off the signed papers, I saw a new salesgirl wearing expensive Italian pumps. She was visibly expectant.

"Hello, do you need some assist—" Norma turned, unable to finish her question when she laid eyes on me.

There were still so many unfinished questions between us.

"He's not here." She steeled herself, some inner indignity perhaps making her wobble in those heels.

I smiled. There was no need to confront Norma. She hadn't really stolen anything. She just continued to break things, and I knew the wreckage would pile up around her on its own.

"I came to drop these papers off for Dalton. I'm surprised to see you here." The truth was, I wasn't all that surprised. My surreptitious affair with Didier had lasted a night, but somehow Dalton's affections for Norma had taken root.

"Mr. Dalton is helping me out. He's a good man." She straightened when she spoke, using one arm to brace her stomach, as if rallying for internal support.

"Well, I'm sure your services will come in handy around here."

She gazed at me, uncertain if I had just delivered a compliment or a jab. I offered her the envelope.

"I—I didn't mean to hurt anyone." Tears welled in her dark eyes.

"We all get what we deserve, Norma. All of us."

Her cindered stare followed me as I exited the shop. Maybe we were both thinking the same thing: How a child, whether desired or miscarried or rescued from war, could turn everyone's lives inside-out.

As I made my way through the masses of hardworking people, it occurred to me that Norma's forecast had come true: One day, she might have my life. At the time, I railed at the mere suggestion. But in the end, she got everything she wanted—a good job, a good man to look after her, and a baby.

And yet, the truth was that I didn't want that life anymore. Norma could have it. She could wear the glass slipper and the fancy foreign shoes and step cautiously from one symbol of entitlement to another without ever having earned a thing. I was certain that her own missteps would soon catch up with her. They always did.

I took a long, deep breath of fetid but promising Manhattan air. The ongoing fiction of my life with Dalton had come to an end. For the first time in a long while, I could live honestly. Being a single mom in a small Manhattan apartment was not a punishment. No doubt, Shari Miller and my Scarsdale neighbors would view it that way. But they were wrong. It was simply the precious cost of freedom.

As I crossed the hectic midtown street, a gust of wind urged me forward, carrying the scent of fallen, wet leaves in its wake. It was autumn in New York and it didn't matter how many things were dying in front of me. Marriages terminated, love affairs gone, fetuses lost, hopes shredded into something less fearful. Because sometimes in life's spectacular displays of loss, true colors emerged.

Park Avenue radiated with orange and yellow and red—shades that burned and faded and fell as quickly as love itself. Nature went unbridled, passions flared, then fizzled. We all lived in the midst of hedonistic displays of life and death and new beginnings. It was a pattern as old as time, but came by surprise in spite of its rigor, like full moons and menstrual cycles.

Dalton, Norma, Didier, and Francine had each found their missing piece. In a way, Jacqui and Martin did too. But for me, the forces controlling my physical and emotional worlds had shifted. Nature had shifted.

I paused considering my new perspectives, my options. I was, after all, in the center of my life. From here, I could picture someone who dove into the sea alone at midnight, leaped from foreign cliffs, slept naked on sun-baked rocks, and let love radically alter her course. From where I stood, I sensed, in all likelihood, the reemergence of someone who just might do it all again.

ACKNOWLEDGEMENTS

I'd like to thank my family, both real and fictional, for years of holding out hope for me as a novelist. Sorry to make you wait so long. Deepest gratitude goes to my chief patron, Alejandro Treviño, who gave me all the time and support I needed from the moment I pulled the trigger and began to write. I'm grateful to the learned Ken Rotcop who completely stepped out of his genre to read my chapters and give good notes. Many thanks to Linda Abrams for her steady enthusiasm and careful reading of my manuscript, and to Janice Gitterman for being a true friend who was quick to read and respond. I also want to thank my longtime buddies Jo Maeder and Ken Kirsh for wise counsel about publishing and for lighting the way. Many thanks also go to the fine women at The Editorial Department (Liz Felix, Morgana Gallaway, Shannon Roberts and Jane Ryder) for their myriad services and support, and to Dane Swanepoel for her artistic energy and fine designs. I also feel truly indebted to Angela Shirley for all manner of author assistance in getting this book out, to Richard Klin for superstar proofreading and to Linda Reilly for being a loving supporter and grammar guru. And to my sister Maria, my mother Gerri and my sons, Amadeo and Ariano, thank you for being my unconditional biggest fans.

Lastly, I'd like to give a nod to New York and France, two places that will always be home to me and will surely engender many more stories to come. And though I have lived rich lives in the metropolises of those great places, suburbia has found me and offered me an observation tower from which to see, appreciate and experience humanity in all of its neighborly and un-neighborly ways. Being outside of the urban periphery has been an unexpectedly inspiring and worthy journey—and one that has fully colored this book.

CPSIA information can be obtained at www.ICGtesting.com
Printed in the USA
LVOW12s1745170615

442816LV00005B/513/P